THE FINAL HARVEST

Gary W. Babb

THE FINAL HARVEST

DOUBLE DRAGON

Chapter 1
The Prophet

"What? You want me to do *what*? Janet, I'm a minister, not a psychiatrist!"

Bill Parks graduated from the seminary only two years earlier and took an offer from a small church in a rural farming/ranching community in the Texas panhandle. As with most ministers, he was on-call from the local hospital to administer spiritual council to those in need. When he received Dr. Janet Mercer's call from the hospital he immediately assumed someone was in need. He did not expect what she asked him to do.

"Mr. Parks, can you come over to the hospital and advise me on a patient? He looks like he is in a trance and is speaking in 'tongues', at least it sounds like it. I hear him talking about God, anyway." After I made my previous response, she continued, "Really, Mr. Parks , I have no idea what I'm dealing with here. An ambulance brought him in from his farm. He apparently went into a trance and his family freaked out and called the emergency line. Now he is here at the hospital, and I don't have any idea what's wrong. At least come take a look and see if you can make any sense out of his rambling."

Apex was a small town, so he knew Janet Mercer, hell you knew most everyone, or at least seen them. He had made it a point to meet and know about Janet, but truth be told, he wished he knew her much better. Neither of them were married, and he thought it kind of made sense for them to gravitate toward each other. They were both around the same age and both of them were relative outsiders, having relocated to Apex because of professional job openings. He came to replace a minister that was retiring, and Janet was recruited to be the resident doctor at the Apex Hospital.

As typical for a small, farming town, the tallest structures are a grain elevator and a water-tower projecting into the sky with APEX written on the side of the elevator and on the top ball of the water-tower, both naming the town. Apex was, however, large enough to have a Baptist church and a hospital, although both were on the small side. The hospital was a fully functioning hospital, but it was single story and minimally equipped.

Both Janet and he were isolated in an unfamiliar town and alone. Most everyone else had been born and raised here, and it had been difficult for them to be accepted in the community. So far they had both been overwhelmed with their new professional responsibilities and hadn't had much time to socialize or worry about being outsiders. Janet's call was the first real opportunity to get together. It was a strange request, but one he was happy to help with.

Bill left immediately and drove the few blocks to the hospital. The sun was just setting as he pulled into the parking lot. When he entered into the emergency room entrance, he was greeted by the nurse/receptionist and directed toward the emergency room.

As he neared the emergency room he could hear a deep monotone voice coming from behind the sliding curtains. The words were unclear, not mumbled but echoing a strange accent. The words were obviously in English, but the heavy accent sounded like Hebrew he had heard from tapes in seminary. But, the accent sounded more pronounced … more ancient.

When he slipped past the screen he saw the patient. He was a muscular man of about fifty, rugged and tanned, obviously a farmer. He was still in soiled coveralls. A heavy stubble of greying beard covered his cheeks and chin, but what caught his attention was the stare. The man's eyes appeared to be focused on something far, far away, seemingly a distance beyond measurement. Bill had seen him before and even talked to him in passing. He remembered the man having a pronounced accent, but it was more of a slow Texas draw, nothing like what he was now hearing.

Janet looked around at him and said, "Hi Reverend Parks. Thanks for coming over."

"Bill. Just call me Bill." He didn't feel like he was here in a formal capacity as a minister.

"Thanks, Bill. I wanted you to meet Mr. Harper and see and hear his symptoms. I don't think I could explain them to another without them having witnessed them. This is just something that must be seen and heard. It's like he is in a trance and isn't aware we are even here. What do you make of this."

Bill, still shocked, said, "Has this happened before?"

A frantic Mrs. Harper said, "We have been married thirty-two years and this has never happened before…ever."

"His accent is definitely a dialect of Hebrew. Is he by any chance Jewish?"

Mrs. Harper said, "Jewish? Are you kidding me? No way! Irish, his grandparents came directly from Ireland, and he is third generation Texan. We have lived on our farm for twenty-five years."

Janet said, "See what I mean? This doesn't make sense, any of it."

This really had his attention now, and Bill turned his focus toward the actual words being spoken. He concentrated on trying to sift through the heavy accent to identify the English words. The monotone cadence made it more difficult. Some words were easily understood, and the more he concentrated, he began to decipher additional words. He heard isolated and random words like: God, Harvest, Render, Fire, Alien, Destroy, Judgement, End of Time, and others.

Bill said, "Are you by any chance taping this so we can analyze it later?"

Janet said, "Yes, both video and audio. I set it up after he came in, and I saw what I was dealing with."

"Great! It will take some time, but I think with a little practice I will be able to understand it. It's just a matter of getting past the accent."

Bill looked intently into Mr. Harper's unfocused eyes and loudly said, "What is your name." He tried to mimic the accent, somewhat successfully."

Suddenly, Mr. Harper went silent, and his eyes refocused to look directly at him. He spoke more clearly saying, "One of my names is Abraham." His eyes then lost their focus, but he remained silent.

All in the emergency room passed shocked looks back and forth.

Bill asked, "One of your names? How many names do you have?"

Again the eyes focused and Abraham said, "This soul has many lives and names. Souls never die, they pass on and join with others. This is God's design, why he created us. These souls are what God is coming to retrieve."

Bill couldn't believe what he was hearing, but then he could. The scriptures taught some of the same thing in a different way. Still, the situation as presented was so bazaar. For once he was speechless.

Janet said, "I waited for you to get here to see this for yourself, but I need to sedate Mr. Harper. I'm hoping when he wakes up he will be normal, like rebooting a computer."

Bill nodded, and Janet injected Mr. Harper. Soon his head began to nod and Janet lay him back on the bed. After Mr. Harper was asleep, she turned to Bill and said, "Thank you for coming over. I appreciate it. I'll get you the recordings if you want to analyzing them."

"Yes, I would love to analyze them. I'll take off now and go through them when I get home. Drop by my house when your shift is over if you like. I will probably have other thoughts by then."

Janet's heart did a quick flutter. Bill Parks was a handsome man, single, six foot tall with short brown hair and hazel eyes. She had seen him around and knew who he was, she had even admired him from a distance. They had talked but little more than greetings and casual talk about the weather. Bill's name and phone number was listed on the on-call minister list at the hospital, and she wanted an opinion from a minister, who just happened to be Bill. She was pleased that it was Bill.

Janet's social life was nonexistent since accepting the resident MD position at the hospital. That had been a year and a half ago, and her duties took all her time so far. Now, with Bill's invitation, her mind began to fill with nonprofessional thoughts, even in light of this medical challenge. She said, "I get off at midnight. Is that too late?"

"Not at all. I'll be up late working on these tapes."

As he was driving home he realized he hadn't given her his address, but she hadn't asked, either. So, she must already know the address, certainly she had his cell number if she needed to call for direction. Finally, they were going to meet, and he was excited.

Most of the audio could be heard clearly from the video tape, so he spent little time on the audio tape. He did, however, send the audio version to one of his seminary professor at the University of Oklahoma, explaining the situation and asking him if he could identify the accent or dialect of Mr. Harper's ranting.

He had just about finished reviewing the tape for the second time when he heard a knock on his front door. He quickly glanced at his clock and smiled to himself. It was fifteen past 12:00am, it had to be Janet. She had changed clothing, well maybe she had just removed her doctor's smock, but she looked different, very different, standing in his doorway She was actually beautiful standing in the light radiating from his living room. The light accented her long blond hair and sparkling blue eyes, and she was smiling...at him. He almost melted in her gaze, and the fragrance of the perfume she had obviously applied pulled at his nostrils.

Bill visibly shook his head, forcing himself to refocus. Bill said, "I'm glad you're here. I have been able to understand much more of Mr. Harper's rambling." He stopped suddenly, realizing his mistake. "Oh, I'm sorry. Please come in. I have fresh coffee."

11

"Thank you, Bill. Coffee would be fantastic." As they sat and began to sip their coffee, she asked, "Is his rambling as crazy as it sounded?"

"Even more so. After I listened for a while and got used to the accent it became easier to decipher. Mr. Harper is telling a story, but obviously not his own. Someone else is telling the story and is relating to a time from ancient history, really ancient, from a time of another's life. Actually, very few were alive from this person's recollection. The story is being told by Abraham, if we can believe it. He doesn't say who he is, but, according to him, he was there when an entity calling itself God visited Earth and planted the seeds of human male and female. Maybe Abraham was one of the males God planted. Abraham tells of God's instruction to him: Be fruitful and multiply."

"According to Abraham, God needs to feed on souls and has done so many times before and in many places. It seems God cannot create a soul (life force). The spark of life (the soul) is created by the joining of a male and female when they produce offspring. This process creates a new soul, which is nourished by living and gaining experiences, knowledge, memories, emotions … life. According to Abraham, souls are eternal until God himself harvests and refines them; which he is evidently about to do."

"During this harvest God absorbs portions of these souls into himself to merge with others. The portions God absorbs are those he deems important. The remainder of the soul is imprisoned in his

12

consuming fire. I assume we can call it the Good and Bad of the soul."

"This is where it gets really strange, assuming you don't already find this strange. I don't know if you noticed, but another voice and accent spoke on the tape, a later lived person, obviously. I noticed it when the voice mentioned the harvest is now full and ripe."

"I did a little Internet research, and if Earth was a field, a harvest is indeed due. There are approximately 8,000,000,000 (8 billion) people alive today and quickly growing far beyond what can be supported and fed. Now, if we assume Abraham is correct and souls don't die, the number of souls that have been generated on Earth since the beginning would be around 110,000,000,000 (110 billion). That is about 15 souls for every living person. So, projecting a harvest time in the future, the time would have to be now or very soon, before the population starts to quickly die off from the effects of overpopulation such as diseases, severe famine, war with massive deaths, etc. ." Bill stopped talking and waited for a reaction.

Janet said, "Wow! You have really gotten into this. It sounds like you believe it."

"Let's just say, the basic concept is based upon biblical teachings that are consistent in almost every known religion. Besides, we have to consider the information presented, not to mention the trance, accent and content. So, let's just say, I am interested in knowing more. Aren't you?"

"Well, it certainly is strange indeed. That's why I called you. I wanted you to hear it for yourself, but I don't consider it an epiphany like it sounds like you do."

Bill was certainly getting excited about what he was discovering, but realized he might be getting overly excited. He didn't want to sound like a religious zealot and scare her away, not when he seemed to be making some headway with her. After all, she did come to his home.

Bill asked, "How is Mr. Harper? Is he still in a trance?"

Janet said, "When I gave him a sedative he went out. He will sleep for many hours. Hopefully, he will be himself when he wakes up. I told the attending nurse to call me when he showed signs of waking up, and I'll go back in to check on him. Want to come with me?"

"Sure, I'm curious. Just give me a call, and I'll meet you there." Janet nodded.

They were continuing to sip their coffee and talk casually about their lives here in Apex, when the call came in. He looked and saw that it was his OU seminary professor. He found that strange, since it was 2:00am. He looked at Janet and told her who it was.

"Hey, Bill, this is Dr. Simpson from OU."

"Hey Phil, I recognize your voice. I've listened to it for years. Remember? I assume you are calling about the tape I sent you? I have Dr. Mercer with me, she is Mr. Harper's physician. Do you mind if I put you a speaker?" Dr. Simpson

14

apparently agreed and Bill lay his phone between him and Janet on the table.

Dr. Simpson said, "Of course this call is about that tape you sent me. I don't mind telling you, that recording has been a major source of discussion for the last few hours. It's gone viral on the Internet."

Janet said, "Viral? You have got to be kidding me. Why?"

"The consensus of opinion around here and other's feed-back is that the accent of the person talking is from the ancient Canaanite era somewhere between 1200 - 586 BC. This dialect of the Hebrew language is long extinct, but some of our linguists swear that by the use of some words and the way they are pronounced that this is the accent detected. The second English language being used in this tape has the scholars puzzled. Some of the words used come from medieval England. By all rights these two languages shouldn't be used together. These languages would have been separated by far too great a distance and the low population of that day would drastically reduce the odds even more. It doesn't make sense."

"We have only begun to address and discuss the actual story this Mr. Harper is telling. It's amazing and will be, I'm sure, a topic for many lengthy discussions. Is Mr. Harper still talking from his trance?"

Janet said, "We won't know until he wakes up from the sedative I gave him. I hoping, for his sake, that he will be normal again."

"Well, we would definitely like to be kept in the loop if you don't mind."

Bill said, "I can give you the video report I have and provide another report by tomorrow evening."

They ended the conversation with agreements to keep each other informed.

Janet looked at Bill with renewed interest and said, "They seem very excited about this situation, as much as you. What they had to say about the accent and its origination is shocking, to say the least. I guess it is hard to explain. I guess you now have my interest, too. But, I hope you understand, my primary focus is helping Mr. Harper, not the research."

"Of course. I understand." Janet seemed to be satisfied with Bill's response, and they settled down to a normal (non Mr. Harper) conversation. They had another cup of coffee, then Janet excused herself to go get some rest. He decided to do the same.

After a late night, Bill was still asleep when Janet called. He quickly jumped up wide awake when he noticed the call was from Janet.

Bill quickly answered and Janet said, "Good morning, Bill." He thought using his first name was a good sign. "I had to come in early, because Mr. Harper woke up earlier than expected. His reboot worked and he is back to normal … almost. He doesn't remember the episode at all, and had no idea why he was here at the hospital. But, and you will find this very interesting, Abraham is still with him. In fact Abraham asked for you. Abraham is not in total control, like he was initially. Mr. Harper is aware of Abraham now, and seems to know or accepts him, at least he didn't freak out when Abraham spoke through him. As it was last night, the heavy accent returns when Abraham speaks."

Bill said, "You said he asked for me?"

"Oh, sorry. Yes, he wants you to come see him, something about you having more questions to ask."

Bill's emotions got the best of him and he blurted, "You bet your ass I do. I will be in as soon as possible. Thanks for calling, Janet."

As he was speeding toward the hospital, he laughed, thinking that that was the fastest he ever showered, shaved, and dressed. His car slid into the closest parking spot, pleased that the local police wouldn't have believed it was him driving like that. Bill ran through the emergency room doors and into the area with the sliding curtains, but the room was empty. Backtracking his route, he stopped at the check-in desk for Mr. Harper.

The nurse immediately said, "They are waiting for you in Room 130." Pointing down the hall. "We needed the emergency room and Dr. Mercer wanted the privacy."

Bill nodded his understanding, said, "Thank you" and rushed in the direction the nurse had pointed. He stopped outside the room to catch his breath, then entered through the open door.

Janet quickly said, "Hi Bill. That was quick." Bill just nodded, still out of breath.

Mr. Harper said, "Thanks, Rev. Parks. Abraham told me about you, and believed you had additional questions for him."

Bill said, "You know about Abraham?"

"Yes, he explained who and what he is, but he really didn't have to. He has always existed in the back of my mind. I now understand and accept the sharing of our souls."

"I wished I did. I listened to the tape Janet shared, and I still don't understand what's happening."

Mr. Harper's eyes glazed over but remained focused upon Bill. His slow tone suddenly turned deep and heavily accented and said, "I understand the technology of the tape recordings from others among us, and I thought, as a minister, you would be quicker to grasp the purpose of my appearance. I will just state the obvious. I am a 'Prophet of God.' I am not the only one. Other Prophets around the planet are also currently making themselves known. We have been here since the beginning of life on this planet … waiting. We are here to prepare the world for the Harvest. It is coming soon and there is nothing anyone can do about it. God will retrieve and refine his souls."

Bill said, "There are numerous religions all over the world that have been preparing the inhabitants of Earth for the Harvest and preaching the teachings of God for thousands of years. Why do we need Prophets now?"

18

For the first time Abraham laughed out loud, a tinkling blast of merriment. After a moment he continued, "None of these so-called religions have any concept of who God is, what he wants, and the real purpose of life. God knows all and knew exactly what religions would teach and how humans would corrupt his teaching over the thousands of years you mention. I'm sure some of what is being taught remains correct, but I'm just as sure that the message has also been added to, subtracted from, and corrupted through the ages. God's true message is short, but humans have turned it into massive volumes of His teachings. Some is a correct assumption, but most is someone else's opinion of what they thought he meant. We are here to relay his true desires and instructions uncorrupted as he intended."

Bill said, "Janet, are you recording this again?" She nodded.

"Alright, Abraham. Maybe you should tell us who God is as you understand him/her/it to be."

Abraham said, "Now that is an intelligent suggestion, one which I will address. God is the sum of souls gathered since the beginning. Each Harvest merges its energy, souls, experiences, memories, and knowledge with God, nourishing him and becoming a part of Him. God continues to expand with the addition of each Harvest. He knows all because He is all. Everything that has ever been is now part of Him, and now He is coming to absorb the souls on this planet."

"How long has God lived?"

19

"You still don't understand. God is not limited by time. God is God, the supreme being, the essence of all. There is no other way to explain Him. He has always been and will always be. Time does not exist for God. God is omnipresent because He is omni-time from your viewpoint. God created time to limit human physical life, but the soul is timeless. Souls are like God, they are eternal and will become part of Him."

"Why does God want to limit human life?"

"God once created thousands of eternal Angels but they had no souls to harvest. God cannot absorb the Angels. They are eternal, therefore they serve Him instead as His messengers and soldiers. To create souls requires the generation of life, the spark of life creates the eternal soul, but the body is not necessary or required, other than gaining the experiences of life. Time was created to limit the body, so God would not have to deal with additional eternal bodies, like the Angels."

"Are all souls to be harvested?"

Mr. Harper eyes widened and a slow smile spread across his face. He said, "You ask interesting questions, but these are questions God wants asked. The answer is, 'Yes'. All souls will be harvested but not like how you might think. The eternal souls will be refined like metal in fire. God only wants the good portion of the soul and not the evil. God is love and all things good. He wants no evil to corrupt his spirit. So, only the good portion of the soul will be absorbed. The evil portion will be refined out and confined in a prison of fire, since it can't be destroyed."

"A soul, the thinking being of consciousness … who you are, will be pulled apart. If more of you is good, the aware soul, thinking portion, will be part of God. If the evil portion dominates, the aware portion gets cast into the fire; but God will still consume what good exists within himself, but it won't think. I believe you get the idea."

Bill asked, "How do you define evil without defined teaching of good and evil?"

"Souls are created with the internal knowledge of what's right and wrong. It is the individual choices that determines the direction and polarity of the soul. Everyone knows what is good or bad when they make their choice."

"I think this is enough questions for now. Mr. Harper needs rest, but you may come back tomorrow if you like, after you analyze what has been said." He was then gone and Mr. Harper returned.

Bill stood, silent in deep thought. He had no idea what to say. So much was running through his mind, and he didn't know what to believe about Abraham and his message.

Mr. Harper shocked him when he spoke, "Do you believe Abraham? I hope you do, because he is trying to help us."

"You know what he said?"

"Yes, we are joined together now. Abraham has always been with me, and we have always been joined, but I just didn't realize it. I resisted him before, but now that he has surfaced we are together."

Bill said, "Well, I suppose I should go and let you rest, but if you don't mind, I will come back tomorrow."

Mr. Harper nodded and held his rough and calloused hand out to shake his and said, "You are welcome Rev. Parks, and it is nice to meet you." Bill nodded.

Bill took his hand and felt the strength of years of hard work radiate through his hand.

As Bill turned to leave, he said, "Dr. Mercer, I think you probably missed breakfast. Want to go get some now? My treat."

Janet smiled and nodded, picked up her phone she was using to record the session, and followed Bill out. Janet casually hooked her arm under his, which startled Bill but quickly turned into a broad smile. Janet said, "You know this is beyond my understanding and ability to treat. I need a psychiatrist to analyze Mr. Harper. Maybe he can figure out what's wrong."

"What if there is nothing wrong with him? What if Abraham is what he says he is, a Prophet?"

Janet suddenly stopped, look up at him and said, "Don't tell me you believe all this crap he is spouting. Do you? I think this is classic case of multiple-personalities."

Bill said, "Hon, I really don't know what I think at this point." Shocked at himself, Bill thought, *Oh, no. Did I really just call her Hon?* He had let that slip, but Janet didn't seem to catch it. He continued, "I can't explain or get passed the ancient accent. That's why I am sharing the interviews with my theology professor."

"Speaking of the recording, let me see your phone, and I will e-mail it to myself and Dr. Simpson."

Oh yes, she heard Bill's slip of the tongue. He apparently liked her. This made her stomach run through a quiver. She hadn't been in a relationship since she moved to Apex, and hardly any in college. She had remained primarily focused on her education. Hell, she hadn't even dated in over two years. She had devoted all of her time here building a relationship with her position at the hospital, but this was going well now and stable. She was ready for a relationship with the right guy, and Bill could be that person.

Janet followed Bill to his car and got in the passenger's seat beside him, and as she buckled up her seatbelt, said, "Bill, did you just call me 'Hon' back in the hospital?" Bill laughed out loud … busted. His face flushed red. She laughed in return and quickly said, "Don't panic, it's OK. Actually, I thought it was cute, and I like you, too."

After breaking the ice with each other, their conversation over breakfast turned more intimate and comfortable. They learned about each other's lives, where they were raised, schools they attended, goals and family. Ironically, while Bill came from a small town in Oklahoma, Janet came from a small town in Texas; but they had shared a year at the University of Oklahoma. Even though they attended the same university, they had never met. This in itself was not surprising, since the campus was huge. Their conversation remained centered upon each other's interests. They didn't even talk about the elephant in the room, Mr. Harper. Of course, other customers in the busy restaurant saw them together and even some of his congregation and Janet's patients dropped by to say, "Hi", obviously being nosy.

Bill leaned closer to Janet and whispered, "I guess we are officially an item now, and I bet we will be the talk of the town by evening, but at least they seem to approve."

"I don't think we will give them much of a choice. Do you?" Bill just grinned.

As they were getting back in his car his phone rang. He looked and said, "It's Dr. Simpson. I wonder why he is calling so soon?"

When Bill answered Janet heard him say, "Yeah, Dr. Mercer is here with me. I'll put you on speaker."

Dr. Simpson sounded stressed and said, "Dr. Mercer, I and my other associates received your latest session with Mr. Harper. It's very interesting, although we haven't analyzed it yet. One item in Mr. Harper's statement, telling us that there are other Prophets, brought up a serious concern."

"We share information in a group of interconnected links around the world. Something surfaced almost immediately about additional Prophets. One of our members, apparently from the Mideast, posted that he had been researching another report about an instance similar to Mr. Harper. Well, this member reported that this so-called Prophet was beheaded. That's all I know so far, but I wanted to contact you immediately so you can get some security around Mr. Harper. I would do so immediately, because the videos are going viral across the Internet. You know how the world is today. It only takes one crazy, and this subject will likely become extremely controversial."

Janet said, "Oh my, this *is* disturbing. Thanks for letting me know. I will get security to the hospital immediately. Thanks again."

Dr. Simpson said, "Bill, once we have a chance to review this latest video I'll call you."

"Great, any time, well, I have church service tonight, but I'll be available afterward."

Janet was already on the phone talking with Sheriff McKinney, explaining the situation and requesting security for Mr. Harper.

When Janet got off her call she said, "This is unbelievable but obviously real. Sheriff McKinney certainly took it as real. He is posting two officers at Mr. Harper's room to keep him safe. Can this all be real? I guess I better get with the program, also. I will call in a psychiatrist to debunk the emerging theories."

Bill said, "I'm not sure what a psychiatrist can do, unless Abraham decides to talk to him directly. And, to answer your question, it's real, because viewers will make it real. Some people will believe anything from wild conspiracy theories to this.

But, what we should be asking ourselves is, 'What if this *is* real, and Abraham *is* a Prophet.'"

"That thought has crossed my mind. I wouldn't know how to handle it as a doctor. You might also be right about the psychiatrist's analysts. I think I better do like Dr. Simpson has done and send the videos out to a network of psychiatrists. Let's see what they come up with."

Bill had just pulled up to the hospital, as Janet finished her comments. Janet smiled and leaned over and kissed him on the lips, and he kissed her back. She smiled again and exited the car. Bill watched her swaying butt all the way inside the hospital and wondered if some of the sway was intentional.

Rev. Parks spent the rest of the afternoon preparing his sermon for his Wednesday night service, and gave Mr. Harper and Abraham little more thought. As usual, he met the attendees on the front steps of the church, and as he had predicted, received several comments and many knowing smiles from the parishioners. He thought, *"It's none of their business that I might have a girlfriend. I'm entitled to a personal life."* But, he held his comments and maintained his smile, even though it was forced.

As he started the service he noticed there were several new guest, but he didn't read anything into it. That is until someone in the congregation stood up and said, "Rev. Park, what can you tell us about Mr. Harper and Abraham?"

26

The person standing wasn't a member of the church. Suddenly it registered. Dr. Simpson had told him and Janet that the videos had gone viral. Obviously, some in Apex had seen it, probably most, since all in the audience seemed to know what the man was asking and were interested in his answer.

Bill said, "I take it that most of you have seen the videos?" Heads nodded all around. He continued, "Well, to be honest I have no idea what to think. I was called in to witness the sessions at the Apex Hospital and offer my comments, and I am continuing with the sessions. I am a part of a world-wide network of religious leaders analyzing the content. Dr. Mercer is networking with psychiatrists for their opinions, but she hasn't heard back from any." They didn't need to know that she just sent the request out.

One of the congregation said, "I know Mr. Harper. He's not crazy."

"Neither Dr. Mercer nor I are suggesting that he is crazy, but it's something that needs to be ruled out. Remember, this just started last night. It will take some time to make sense of all this."

Another shouted out, "What if he is what he says he is, a Prophet?" Silence filled the auditorium.

Bill was stunned by the turn of events. He hadn't expected to have to address this subject for quite some time. These folks were in a panic, and they needed ... what? Comfort - Assurance - Denial? His sermon now forgotten, he had to quickly analyze what he, personally, believed. He honestly didn't know what he believed, it was far too soon, but he suddenly realized that he hadn't walked away from the situation as being totally absurd. Did that mean part of him believed? Was it believable? Possibly it was, if he accepted it on faith. He accepted Christianity on faith. Is it possible to accept both? Could it be that both were correct?

Silence continued to rest like a weight on the congregation for several long moments, while Bill's mind raced. His face eventually relaxed and resolve formed in his expression. He had made a decision and said, "For the sake of discussion, let's assume this Abraham is real." Gasps could be heard, but no one spoke. "What Abraham has said so far is that a 'Harvest' is coming. Christianity, and most other religions of the world, have been teaching this for thousands of years."

"In the Old Testament, *Revelation 14:15:16 states: And another angel came out of the temple, crying out with a loud voice to Him who sat on the cloud, "Put in your sickle and reap, for the hour to reap has come, because the harvest of the earth is ripe." Then He who sat on the cloud swung His sickle over the earth, and the earth was reaped.*"

"There are many other scriptures that talk about the 'Harvest'. So, what Abraham is telling us is the same. He mentions 'Good & Evil', Christianity teaches the same. Abraham talked about God creating the Angels, Christianity also teaches the same. He said souls are eternal, don't

28

we believe the same? He mentioned souls being refined by fire. The Christian scriptures mention this many times. Are any of these statements bad? I guess I could go on, but what's the point? As I have said, it is far too soon to form an opinion, and I refuse to do so. Let's just continue to listen and research."

Another non-member stood, obviously intent on pushing the subject; but Bill silenced him with a hand pushed toward him and a firm stare. Bill said, "I can tell you are interested in this subject, so this Sunday I will give a full report during the service. I should know more by then. So, tell your friends to attend if they want to know more."

The questions, answers, and unorganized format had eaten up the time, and his statement offering further reports seemed to quell their anxiety for the time being. He said his "Good Byes" on the front steps and breathed a sigh of relief as everyone disappeared.

Chapter 2
The Fallout

Bill remained disturbed by the reaction from his congregation, but he decided to just ignore it for a while. He changed into his gym shorts and T-shirt and settled down to the last Mr. Harper recording and began analyzing it. He was on the third playback when he heard a knock on the door. It was 12:30am. It had to be Janet getting off shift, so he rushed to the door. There she was in all her glory ... smiling.

Janet said, "I'm happy to see that you *can* get comfortable. This is the first time I've seen you without a coat and tie. Now I feel overdressed. I came by for coffee. I hope you have some."

Bill said, "I'm sorry. I wasn't expecting you, but yes, I have coffee." Janet slipped past him and helped herself to the coffee.

Bill turned to watch her. She looked comfortable to be with him, and uncharacteristic for him, he flirted and said, "If you feel overdressed, feel free to take off any thing you like." He almost choked when he realized what he had said. He hadn't meant it to sound so ... so suggestive.

Janet spun around, but she was smiling. She said, "Good for you, Bill. I was wondering if single ministers were prudes. I guess you're human after all. As to your suggestion, I guess we'll see." She then turned back to the coffee bar.

That went well, he thought. He smiled back. He liked her and felt comfortable with her, so much so that he walked up behind her, gently turned her around to face him, and kissed her. When he looked into those liquid pools of deep blue, he was lost in desire. The kiss lingered long and quickly turned passionate. Her arms slipped around him, and pulled him tight to her. He felt her breasts press against his chest. Their breathing began to come in heavy gasps. It was magical. They continued kissing, as Janet pushed Bill backwards toward the couch. She pulled Bill down on top of her as she fell back on the couch. They began frantically pulling the clothing from each other until they merged together completely. Bill and Janet lost all inhibitions, as he sank deep inside her warmth. They were simply two animals intent on sex. They met each other's thrusts with strength and violent passion. Their joint climax came with screams and force.

Afterward, they continued to remain joined, sucking huge lungfuls of air. After they had calmed some, Janet looked deep into his eyes and said, "I don't feel so overdressed now."

Bill burst out laughing, a truly joyful release, then he said, "I'm pleased that you feel comfortable. Let's not get you dressed. I'd hate for you to feel uncomfortable again." It was Janet's turn to laugh.

Janet said, "That was exactly my thought. But, I really need to take a shower, and borrow a T-shirt for later."

"Much later, Hon. And, you are sure sweaty, so I better help you get clean in the shower."

Janet smiled really big and said, "It's amazing how we think alike."

After an intimate shower and more passionate love making in Bill's bed, they lay together intertwined in legs and arms. Bill relished in the warmth of Janet's body, and never felt more comfortable with anyone. The scent of her body filled him with that same warmth, and he felt his growing love simmering inside him. How could this be wrong? Still, his congregation would frown upon him for what just happened, but he wouldn't change anything. Why does a church flock demand more from their minister than they require of themselves? Of course it was a sin to have sex out of wedlock, but it seemed so right. Besides, everyone sins, and he was no exception. There was only one sinless person.

Janet twisted in his arms to look at him and said, "What are you thinking?"

I'm thinking that I have never felt happier than I am at this moment."

"I know that feeling well. But, Bill, do you regret it happening? I mean, are you concerned that your church will find out and damn you to hell?"

Bill laughed and said, "Honestly, I do have a concern, but I have strong feeling for you that I'm sure can't be controlled. The big head says restraints is best, but the little head says, 'Fuck her.'" They both burst out in hysterical laughter.

Janet turned serious and said, "I can't explain it, but I have strong feeling for you, too. I have since we first met. If you hadn't made a move tonight, I think I would have. Then again, I might be just horny." They laughed. "You should know, however, that I do have a serious concern. If our relationship continues, like I suspect it might, I'm not sure I can be a minister's wife. I was raised in the church as a child, but I lost my way during my life. That part might require more than I am capable of giving."

Bill was grinning when he said, "What makes you think I want to marry you, anyway?"

Janet laughed and said, "I can tell you love me already, and sooner or later you will ask me to marry you. But, I don't know what I will say, but if I *want* you to and you don't ask me, I *will* have to confess my sins to your church." Bill grinned, hugely. He couldn't allow that to happen. So, he was positive he *would* ask her to be his wife.

Bill stopped talking and kissed her soft lips, and they were off again riding the lust train.

Afterwards, as they were cuddling, his phone rang. Bill reached for it and after glancing at the screen he said, "It's Dr. Simpson." Bill put the phone on speaker so Janet could hear.

"Hello Phil, you're making a habit of calling in the middle of the night. It must be important."

"Well, yes and no. Most of those in the know are awake on the other side of the world, but it is important."

"We found five other Prophets, at least they claim to be Prophets. One is in India in the middle of Hindu country. The Prophet's host is Hindu. Another is, well was, in Iran. His religion was Islam, and is the one that was beheaded by zealots. I told you about him last night. There is also another in Israel. The host, of course, is of the Jewish faith. There are reports from China about man claiming to be a Prophet. That man's religion is Buddhism. The last one we could identify is a man living in England. He is of the Roman Catholic faith, the largest category of Christianity. So, including Mr. Harper there are evidently six Prophets, well five now, representing the major world religions."

"We find it very telling that they all show up at the same time with similar reports of accents and substance. I added your e-mail address to the closed network list, so you will be able to follow all the reports coming in. Even though the network is a closed, the information is still making it public. Bill, there are millions of hits on that link. It's unbelievable."

"Bill, you asked some very good questions and received excellent answers from Abraham. Those are currently being analyzed by theologians around the world. He only allowed for few questions, and we are anxious for your next session. When will that be?"

"I will meet again with him after I get some sleep, probably around noon. I will forward the video afterwards."

Phil said, "I hope you don't mind, but we are receiving suggested questions from the network you might consider. Some of them are quite good. I'll forward them to you as a separate file, since there are a lot of hits."

Bill said, "I had my Wednesday service earlier tonight, and the congregation already knew about the sessions, plus we had many extras show up. I never got to my planned sermon. They seemed to be panicking some. I promised to give them a full report on Sunday, which seemed to pacify them. But, Sunday might get a little wild."

"I'm afraid that will happen, probably on a much larger scale, also. I believe most Christians will take the news as a motivator to return to the church and the faith, but I also believe there will be radicals surface on both ends of the spectrum. That's the buzz within the network. We've already seen it happen in Iran. But, all we can do is continue to follow Mr. Harper and the others and see where it goes."

"Bill, do you need some help there?"

"Not right now, I'll let you know if I do. Right now I just need some sleep. I'll talk to you tomorrow."

While Bill was talking to Phil, Janet received a phone call and quickly ran into the living room to take it. She was returning now, but he had to laugh, because she was still very naked. She jumped back in bed, snuggled up close, and quickly pulled the sheet over her chilled body. Bill waited,

35

knowing the expression on her face indicated concern.

Janet said, "This situation is really getting serious. Sheriff McKinney just called to tell me that a crowd, both supportive and hostile, is gathering at the hospital, and he thinks he might have to move Mr. Harper to a more secure location. I have no idea where that might be."

Bill said, "Well, I guess we aren't going to get any sleep tonight. We should go to the hospital and see what we can do to help." Janet nodded.

When they pulled up at the Emergency Entrance at 5:00am, they couldn't believe what that saw. The first indication of a pending surprise came with a very full parking area. There were even cars lining both sides of the street. Janet, however, had her own private parking slot that was, thankfully, still unoccupied. Bill parked his car in her slot, which was close to the entrance. There was a large crowd of people gathered, but the next major surprise was a large white TV remote van blocking part of the entrance. The side of the van was stenciled in large, red letters with: KFDA TV, NewsChannel 10, Amarillo, TX.

Janet said, "Surely this activity is not about Mr. Harper."

Bill's eyebrows rose, and he nodded and said, "I believe it is, Janet. Phil said the videos are going viral on the Internet."

They apparently were recognized from the Internet videos. As they neared the entrance, they were immediately mobbed by the crowd and reporters with video cameras blocking their way. Everyone began firing questions so loud and fast they couldn't be understood. They weren't prepared for this and didn't know what to do. They were surrounded and couldn't get through or retreat. They were captured within the closing mob of people.

Thankfully, they heard Sheriff McKinney's voice over a loudspeaker telling the crowd to disperse and make room. Soon there were two deputies pushing their way through the crowd, pulling and ushering Bill and Janet toward and into the entrance and safely behind a line of police officers, neither of them recognized.

They were still somewhat in shock at what had and was happening. Sheriff McKinney reached them and said, "This is building too fast. I had to call in for help, and thankfully law enforcement officers are coming in from all around. Still, I hear many others are en route to here. We can't maintain security here. We have to move him soon."

Janet said, "He doesn't really need any more medical treatment. Actually, I could release him."

Sheriff McKinney said, "I'm sorry, Janet, but you can't just release him into the middle of all this chaos. You just saw what they are capable of. They would mob him in this feeding frenzy. We have to take him somewhere safe, at least for a while."

"Yes, of course, but where?"

"My next level is the State Police, but I'm also thinking federal. I'll make some calls. This is still growing fast and likely to get much larger."

"Whatever you want, as soon as you want. I'll sign off on it. I'll go tell him and release him."

It was easy to identify the room Mr. Harper was in by the guards standing outside. Bill and Janet walked in, and Janet immediately mounted her phone to start the recording. She then took the clipboard to review his medical charts.

After a moment of reviewing the charts she said, "Good morning, Mr. Harper. How are you feeling?"

Mr. Harper said, "Well, I feel like a prisoner with these policemen at my door, but otherwise I feel good."

Janet said, "They are hear for your protection. I'm sorry to say that the recordings have gone out on the Internet and the world is hanging on every word you and Abraham have said. The crowd and media are acting kind of crazy and wanting to interview you. It's just too overwhelming to expose you to that right now. You can't see from here, but there is a large crowd outside. The Sheriff wants to transfer you to a more secure facility. He is setting that up right now. Again, it is for your protection."

"Yes, I know about the attention I'm getting. I've watched it on the television." pointing.

They turned in the direction of his point and saw the gathering outside on his television. Some talking head was in the middle of the screen with the crowd video playing in the background. The caption also said, God's Prophet.

Mr. Harper continued, "God's timing of selecting now is what he knew would happen, because he already saw it. Earlier than now it would have taken many years to get his word out. Today, it has only taken days, and the entire world is listening. Now they need to comply with his word."

Bill was curious and said, "Are you now speaking for Abraham?"

"Yes, we are one now in most things, but he may yet speak. There is more to be said and it needs to come from God's Prophet."

"Rev. Parks, do you have more questions?"

Bill laughed and said, "Oh my, yes, but let's set up the video first." Janet nodded and started her camera. "I may never run out of questions, but there *is* one that came to mind after our talks. If God is an all-powerful God, why can't he create a soul?"

Abraham surfaced and said, "You are wasting precious time with a senseless question. God does create souls. You have a soul, because God made male and female in order to create a soul. You want to squabble over His methods?"

"Sorry, it just didn't make sense to me, and I thought to clarify the statement."

"Who is the Devil?"

Abraham, through Mr. Harper, sighed and a tightened expression flashed across Mr. Harper's face, obviously frustration. He said, "The Devil,

Satan, Lucifer, whatever you wish to call him is one of the eternal Angel gone bad. He can't be destroyed, so God keeps him and his followers isolated. I'm answering your question, but Satan is not important. The world should only be concerned with God. Please try to limit your questions, because my time is short."

"I understand. Here is a question that is important to us. Why are there five Prophets?"

"Good question and one God wants explained. There are actually six major religions of this world, each one claiming to know the absolute words of God. This is the corruption I mentioned previously. There is only one God and one accurate description of his word, and this is what we are here to provide ... for the last time. His word is far simpler than various religions have made of it. You have received most of his instructions already. These Prophets are here to spread his message within the various so-called major religions and languages. The five major religions are: Buddhism, Christianity, Hinduism, Islam, and Judaism. Christianity has two major division, one being Roman Catholic. God provided a Prophet solely for them, because it is a larger group he wanted to address. As you probably already know, the Prophet for Islam has been destroyed, but God wasn't counting on that Prophet to project much information. That religion doesn't accept much outside information, but some of the message will make it to the masses through the other Prophets. The word is already spreading."

"What do you mean by preparing the world for the Harvest?"

"Now that is a meat and potatoes question, the main one. Our message is 'Prepare yourself for the Harvest'. As I have already told you, God is coming to reap his Harvest of only the good things. Evil is summarily rejected. Prepare yourself by purging yourself of evil. Replace it by doing good, so your thinking soul, who you are, will reside with God and not in the burning fire. Do good now and stop doing evil, while you can, before it is too late. Nourish your soul with good. This is the main message we are here to relay. Some will heed this message, while others will continue, even heighten, their evil ways. The population of this planet will polarize into good and evil as a result of this message. This is part of the refining process."

Bill's thoughts turned inward to something he had been thinking and asked, "Is there a Heaven? If so, what's it like being there?"

Of course there is a Heaven. Heaven is God. Being with God makes all things possible. Whatever you're thinking mind can conceive is possible with God. As an example, if you want to fish, ski, visit with family, etc. all you have to do is think about it and it is so, but the other advantages can't be explained in terms you can currently understand. All this is possible as long as your thinking mind is active with God."

Abraham, now thick with accent, said, "My time is done, now. I will go dormant now and will be able to answer no more questions. The world

41

has received all that God wished known. Now it is up to each person to comply … or not." Abraham drifted away, back into Mr. Harper soul.

Bill, said, "But I have many more questions."

Mr. Harper said, "I'm sorry, but Abraham is gone. I no longer sense him with me."

Bill said, "Damn! I should have asked more intelligent questions."

Janet said, "You asked very good questions. I think Abraham just provided all the information he was assigned to provide. I think your last question provided that opportunity."

"I think I better go tell Sheriff McKinney about the change. I don't think we will need to move Mr. Harper now. I will, however, suggest that he take a vacation away. I'll go make an announcement to the crowd and media and let them know the Prophet is gone, and Mr. Harper has no memory of it. That's a little white lie but mostly true. That should take the pressure off him for a while."

Bill said, "Janet, be careful. Their focus will turn to you, as his doctor. You were present during all the interview sessions. And, of course, they will probably want to interview me also, since I did the interviews." Bill looked at Janet and saw the resolve on her face. She obviously wanted to protect her patient and would. He continued, "So, I guess I will go with you to make the announcement as soon as we forward this last video to Phil." Janet smiled and nodded her thanks.

Janet and Bill found Sheriff McKinney in one of the offices and explained the situation. He agreed with Janet's assessment and led them to the Emergency Entrance and announced to the crowd and media, which had almost doubled since they arrived, that there would be a brief announcement by Mr. Harper's doctor and interviewer. The crowd immediately tightened around the entrance but back from a compacting, heavy line of police officers. The line of cameras and talking heads filling the front of the mass.

Janet stepped forward into their focus and said, "I'm Dr. Mercer, Mr. Harper's doctor. Mr. Harper is stable now. His delusions have ceased, and he has no memory of the incidents. He is unable to address the sessions, so I ask you to leave him alone. As his attending physician, I can offer no explanation for the occurrences of the trance and trance induced rambling or content. As you already know, the sessions were recorded. Somehow, they have found their way on to the Internet, or you wouldn't be here now. I have provided the recordings to a network of psychiatrist, and they are analyzing them now. I'll see if they come up with anything new, but I believe it will remain a mystery. That's really all I have to say."

As she was backing up, one of the reporters bellowed out, "Will you be releasing Mr. Harper now?"

Janet stepped back up and said, "There is no medical reason to keep him, but I don't want him subjected to interrogations. It wouldn't do any good, since he has no memory of the incidents. So,

I will keep him as long as you remain here." Other reporters asked questions, but she ignored them.

The same loud reporter ask, "Rev. Parks, do you believe the Prophet's message?"

Bill stepped up to the microphone and said, "I'm still analyzing what was said, and I haven't come to any conclusions yet. But, I promised my congregation the first, full report on Sunday. If you want to hear that report, come to the Apex Baptist Church on Sunday." Many additional questions were barked out, but they were ignored.

As they were being escorted to his car by police, Janet leaned in and said, "That was a shameless plug for your church."

Bill laughed and said, "It probably was, but I bet Sunday's attendance will be above average. Besides, I owe the news media nothing, and I owe my congregation everything and first. You too, Janet. You will have to come Sunday also to find out what I really think."

Janet laughed and said, "Oh, that's not fair. I bet I can persuade you to tell me before then, but that wouldn't be fair, either." Bill grinned.

Janet asked Bill to take her by her apartment to get a change of clothing, but before they got there they saw news media vehicles outside waiting to ambush her. And, they encountered the same ambush outside his house. So, they decided to drive over to the next, large town, which was Amarillo, and get a motel.

En route they found an open Walmart and purchased a change of clothing and toiletry items for their, hopefully, only overnight stay. Janet smiled as she also modeled a sexy nightgown. As they searched for a secluded motel where they wouldn't be easily found by the media, Janet snuggled up against Bill and kissed him.

Janet whispered in his ear in between nibbles, "You know what, Bill?" She didn't wait for an answer. "I'm falling for you ... big time. What are we going to do about it?"

Hearing those words made Bill's heart flutter, because he was feeling exactly the same. It was like Janet was already part of him, and he liked it. Bill pulled over to the side of the road, took Janet in his arms, and kissed her ... hard and passionately. Bill then said, "Well, my dear, I think we should get married before everyone figures out what's going on with us. We both have to worry about our professional reputations, whether we like it or not. I certainly do not want to stop being with you. As a matter of fact, I want to be with you all the time. Will you marry me? I'm sorry I can't get down on my knees to propose properly, but I do love you. I can't explain it, but it's like we were meant to be together."

Janet said, "This is crazy. You know that don't you? We have only known each other for a few days, but I'm about to say 'Yes', so I guess we are both crazy."

"Yeah, it sounds much better than, 'Let's sneak off to a motel for wild sex.'"

They burst out laughing, which quickly turned into something more.

45

Bill's face shown bright with excitement and said, "Can you call in for a couple of days off? You know Amarillo is a big city. We could probably get all the paperwork done and find a Justice of the Peace to marry us tomorrow, of course we will have to do it again later at my church. The congregation would never forgive me if I exclude them."

Janet smiled hugely. "I like the way you think, another reason I love you." Silence filled the car with those words. This was the first time she had ever used those words and truly meant them. It *was* like they were meant to be together.

"I love you, too." They again fell into a passionate embrace that left them quivering in lust. The search for a motel became their immediate focus.

The motel they quickly found was the first they came upon. It satisfied their immediate needs … it had privacy and a bed! They carried their Walmart bags into the room and quickly discarded them, along with their clothing. Items of clothing went flying in all directions as they made their way to the bed. Both were professing their undying love as they pounded their bodies together and screamed jointly in orgasm. They remained joined as Janet rolled them over so she could control Bill from the top.

Bill had never experienced anything like what Janet subjected him too, but he loved every moment. He was totally engulfed in her steaming hot, velvet sheath, and Janet rode him like a bucking bronco. She owned him, and he never wanted to be without her. Their love was emotional and physical, and he wanted to marry her quickly, before she could change her mind. But, that would never happen, judging by her passion and affection. Their exceptional level of sex could never be experience without the overwhelming emotional attachment to each other, and Bill's insatiable desire and lust for Janet boggled his rational mind. Janet also seemed to have the same problem, if it could be called a problem. This was true love.

Much later they cuddled together, relishing in their joint warmth, and Janet said, "I think we better go eat something. I'm really hungry. I have no idea why."

Bill laughed out loud and said, "I have no idea why, either, but food sounds great. Have you been to the Big Texan restaurant? I've heard a lot about it, but I have never tried it. It is supposed to be one of the best steak houses in this part of the country."

"Yeah, I have heard about it. Let's do it. I could really get into a big T-bone steak, but we need to shower first."

They jumped up together and showered together, making sure each other was clean. They dried each other and dressed in the change of clothes they bought.

As Janet unpacked her Walmart bag she said, "Hey Bill, I bought a really sexy nightgown at Walmart, but I never got a chance to put it on. I will when we get back."

47

"Don't show it to me yet. Wait until after I've had a steak, hon. We might not make it to the restaurant, and I need nourishment. Hey, you're a doctor. Maybe you could write me a prescription to give me strength." He winked and Janet laughed.

Janet said, "Well, I have a lot of years to catch up on."

"Yeah, me too, but we have a lot of time."

After Janet looked at the menu at the Big Texan she smiled and said, "You asked about a prescription for stamina. I noticed they have Mountain Oysters on the appetizer menu. You should try them. They are stocked full of minerals, vitamins and protein, and are considered an aphrodisiac by many."

"Really? I've never heard of them. Oysters? Why do they call them mountain oysters?"

Janet couldn't hold back her mischievous grin and said, "My love, they are bull testicles. If you can get past the thought of what they are, I have heard they are quite tasty, and they are very nutritious for what you asked about. Doctor's orders."

Bill decided to be brave and ordered the appetizer with his T-bone. Janet gave him a raised eyebrow in surprise. He did manage to get past the thought and eat most of them, but had absolutely no problem eating the huge T-bone steak. It was the best and largest steak he had ever eaten, but they were so stuffed when they finished, they had to rest for an hour over coffee, just digesting. The experience was incredible, but not something you would want to do often.

One slightly tense moment came when their food arrived at the table. Bill said, "I hope you don't mind, but I would like to say grace before we eat."

Initially, Janet flashed surprise, then after a moment of thought she said, "Yes, of course. I'm going to be a preacher's wife. I have been thinking about how my life will change. I thought about it hard, but I love you Bill and accept that about you. That's who you are, that's who *we* are now."

Pride of Janet lit up his face, and he said, "That's why I love you. I think God put us together. That's why we clicked so well and are together now. We were meant to be together." Janet smiled.

Just as they reentered their motel room Bill's phone chimed. A quick look showed that it was Phil calling a little earlier than the last few nights, well mornings, actually. Bill answered and clicked on the speaker.

Phil said, "Have you seen the news? If not, you should. You are all over the news wires. CNN has been calling you a charlatan and con man. They claim you started the narrative on the Prophets and are trying to pull off a major hoax on the world just to get new members in your church and make a ton of money from contributions from around the world."

Bill was speechless, his eyes glazed over with shock. So, Janet took over and said, "That's insane and just mean. Why would they tell all those lies?"

Phil said, "Of course it is insane, but the news media doesn't care about facts or the truth. They just want headlines and ratings and don't care who they hurt or destroy to get their way. They make their allegations then provide their fake evidence. Bill invited all to attend his church on Sunday to hear his thoughts about the Prophet. I think it could be a media circus on Sunday. I'm on my way there to help Bill. Is he still speechless?"

"Yeah, pretty much. He is still in shock. We will be back in Apex on Saturday. We are in Amarillo now to get married, and I'm not about to let this crap ruin our very short honeymoon."

"Well, congratulations you two. I hadn't heard."

Janet laughed and said, "Neither had we. Bill just asked me, and I said, 'Yes'. It was a surprise to both of us, too, but when it is meant to be, you have to go with the flow. Phil, I need to go and calm Bill. We'll call you back a little later. OK?"

Bill's eyes were still glazed over, and he had begun muttering to himself. Janet listened, but he made no sense. Janet placed her hands on his cheeks and forced him to look at her. She kissed him and his eyes began to focus on hers. Janet smiled and said, "Hon, don't let the news media control you. I love you, and I know the truth, and I'm with you now."

Bill's tense face slowly relaxed and he smiled and kissed her back. "Thanks, my love. You are all I care about. The news was just shocking to me. I would say that I can't believe it, but then, knowing the media, I can believe it. I guess what is so surprising now is that I'm the victim. I didn't anticipate this turn of events, but it is what it is, and I will stand up for what I believe. The problem is, I'm not sure what I believe."

"Whatever you believe, I will stand up with you. We are one."

Bill suddenly grinned and said, "Hon, will you stand up with me wearing that sexy nightgown?" Bill stopped, laughed, and said, "I don't mean me wearing the nightgown. I mean you wearing it."

Janet laughed, a truly humorous outburst, and said, "You big turd. You got me with that one, and you will also get me again with the nightgown on."

Janet returned from the bathroom in spectacular fashion. Bill could do nothing but stare with his jaw somewhere down on his chin. Janet was beautiful. Her long blond hair cascaded over her shoulders, accenting her beautiful face and contrasting against her liquid blue eyes, that were gently but hungrily looking into his. She had replaced her lipstick on those cupid-bow lips and were already puckered halfway in a kiss. Bill let his eyes take in the rest of her. She was wearing a light pink, see-through nightgown that barely covered her breasts and nether parts but revealed everything. A darker pink lace lined the bottom, breasts and shoulder straps. The pink color of the lace matched the color of her hard, pointing nipples, clearly visible through the virtually transparent nightgown. Bills attention was totally focused on Janet, all other thoughts gone for the moment.

They came together, and Bill picked her up, cradled in his arms. They fell on to the bed in passion, as he explored the nightgown and the treasures beneath.

Later, with the sexy nightgown still gathered around Janet's neck, they lay wrapped in each other's arms. Janet said, "We need to call Phil back. I guess we need to hear more about what's going on around the world and what to expect. I think you're calm enough now. I know I am."

Bill turned serious and said, "No, sweetie. I don't want to hear anything right now, we'll wait until after we are married, tomorrow night. We need to sleep right now. Remember, we didn't sleep last night."

"Oh, is that why I'm so tired?"

Bill laughed and said, "Well, that's part of it."

They were both in agreement and snuggled together and fell into a deep refreshing rest.

Bill was still drowsy when light coming in the window woke him. He smiled at seeing the nightgown crumpled at Janet's waist. The sight of Janet's naked body beneath aroused him, and he began to stroke her thighs.

Janet opened her eyes, smiled and said, "Hey hon. Don't get any ideas. You aren't getting any sex until after we are married and I have a ring on

52

my finger. I'm saving myself for my future husband.

Bill burst out laughing then said, "Well, you better hurry up and get dressed. We need to get married quickly before my sins include rape. It was Janet's turn to laugh.

They had obtained the Marriage License by noon. That had gone well, but the Justice of the Peace was out of town. So, Bill called around and found a minister he knew that would perform the ceremony. They were officially husband and wife by 5:00pm, but since they hadn't eaten all day, they found a Denny's on the way back to their room.

They both had turned off their phones, since they didn't want any interruptions. Their marriage took precedence over any other activities, but while they were eating they both jumped at the mention of their names on the wall TV. They quickly jumped up to get close to the TV speaker and asked the waitress to turn up the volume, which she did.

The reporter was interviewing the Apex Hospital Administrator and, of all people, the head deacon of his church. It was the same aggressive and obnoxious reporter that bellowed out questions during Bill and Janet's comments at the hospital. The reporter was asking them what they thought about the Prophet hoax Bill and Janet were trying to spread through the church and hospital.

The deacon, a man Bill knew well and had always liked, said, "Once the church realized what lies Rev. Parks was trying to spread through our church and his whoring around with Dr. Mercer,

53

we called an emergency meeting and fired him. Our church is a Christian church and we don't want to be associated with any false prophet." The reporter was getting the sensationalism he wanted and turned to the Hospital Administrator.

"I feel much the same. Once we saw your reports of Dr. Mercer and Rev. Parks entering a motel together, we realized that they were much closer than most thought, and there must be a conspiracy being conducted. And, we don't want to be associated in any way with this false conspiracy. We have terminated Dr. Mercer's employment, and she won't be allowed to return to our facility."

Bill and Janet stood in absolute shock after hearing the interviews, which must have been running repeatedly most of the day. Other's in the restaurant were staring at them, but they hardly noticed. Both their legs seemed wobbly, so they sat back down in their booth, staring at each other in total disbelief.

Janet said, "Darling, I'm so sorry I got you involved and got you fired. I'm really, really sorry."

"Well, you got fired, also."

Surprisingly, Janet smiled and said, "Actually, I understand their motivation to distance themselves from a perceived controversy, but it will cost them dearly. I have an iron-clad five year employment contract with the hospital. I have a golden parachute, which they will have to pay. I, we, just got advanced a five-year salary settlement, plus I have some savings. We will be all right, financially."

"I have savings as well, and from what I just heard, I have a potential lawsuit, several, actually; but what I am having trouble with is how fast they turned on me. I thought I had friends there. We are both victims of the media. The most surprising part of all this is I still don't know how to deal with Abraham's message, but I'm beginning to think he is what he said he was. Why else would the evil side attack with such venom, like Abraham said would happen? He said the good and evil would polarize. That appears to be what's happening, but I didn't expect my church would be on the evil side. I will have to do a much better job in the future."

Janet turned serious and said, "I love you all the more. I guess I am becoming a minister's wife, because I agree with you. I believe Abraham! And, I think you should follow your faith and stand up for his message. Maybe God is preparing you to do just that by taking away your job and getting you out from under evil taskmasters."

Janet certainly had Bill attention and he couldn't be more proud of her. God had certainly sent her to him, and he needed her.

Chapter 3
War has been Waged

They waited to turn on their phones until they were back in their room, but as soon as they did, both phones began to ring immediately. Janet left him in the bedroom and took her phone into another room for her calls. Bill's first call was understandably from Phil.

Phil said, "Thank God I finally got you. Are you OK?"

Bill laughed and said, "Well, I got fired from my church, and the devil is attacking me from every direction. Other than that, I'm fine."

"Yeah, I heard that on CNN, but that's what I'm calling about. Don't worry about that. I have a job for you, and I hope you will accept."

"Since I started your interview postings within my Internet network, the whole thing is mushrooming within the religious community, they came together with funds and put me in charge of the Prophet message presentations and defense against the evil organizing and attacking, just like what you are seeing there."

"The religious community is also polarizing. For example: The Roman Catholics, at least the hierarchy, have come out debunking the Prophet. They are calling them False Prophets and the news media is eating it up. Many of the Roman Catholic members, however, are flocking to others, us mostly. We are calling ourselves The Prophet's

Congregation, and this community is coming together more and more. It's crazy, even the non-Christian religions are swarming to us to know more. Plus, because of the Prophets' reference on souls seeming to suggest reincarnation, even the Buddhist are wanting to know more. The masses are afraid. The Prophets' messages have them all thinking the end is near, and, I for one, believe it's true."

"The thing is, Bill, these organizations all want you to address them. Actually, most are demanding that you come. That's why they are pooling their money and pushing it at me, because they know we are friends. Bill, I could send you in a thousand directions. Please tell me you will help me with this. I will get all the organization done and paid for. All you have to do is talk about your experience with the Prophet and his message."

Bill listened without comment, shocked at the world's response. This was happening far too fast.

Janet, returning to the bedroom, had heard most of Phil's comments. Now she was smiling and said, "See, Bill. I told you that God has a plan, and you are part of it. Only God could make this happen this fast. Damn, listen to me. God has made me a minister's wife for sure. Phil, Bill is in shock again, but he will do it." Bill was nodding but said nothing.

Janet said, "Phil, Mr. and Mrs. Parks will come as a team, but not tonight. It's our honeymoon." Bill focused momentarily and grinned at her.

They could hear the relief in Phil's voice when he said, "I'm very pleased to hear this, and congratulations on your marriage. I will let the organization know you accepted and get things started, and I welcome the team approach. That will work out even better ... much better actually. I'll call you when I have more to tell."

When Bill disconnected, Janet said, "I am becoming a believer. I told you so. I believe this *is* the way it is supposed to be, just like Mr. Harper, we have become tools to do God's will."

"Well, maybe you are right. I will do my best to tell those that will listen the truth as I see it."

Bill was interrupted by another call coming in. He answered with the speaker on. "Bill, this is Deacon Jones. I'm glad I caught you. I wanted to make sure you got my voice mail letting you know not to come in to the church on Sunday. We don't want any part of the circus you are creating."

Bill's voice turned cold as ice and he said, "Yeah, I got your message but not on voice mail. I got your message on CNN. I'm trying very hard to turn the other cheek, but when you called my wife a whore ... well, it does make it very difficult. I'm usually not into revenge, but you said some nasty things about her, and the church and you, personally, will be hearing from my attorney about the slander you spouted, and on national television no less."

"Wife? I didn't know you and Dr. Mercer got married."

"Well, now. You didn't ask. Did you? We got married in Amarillo. I thought we were friends, but I'm discovering that you are nothing but a sanctimonious hypocrite. You tossed me aside like old lettuce, but I have a new platform now. You actually did me a favor by firing me."

Deacon Jones began stuttering and finally said, "I'm so sorry, Bill. I just got caught up in the news reports."

"Well, if it's any comfort, I'm suing CNN, too." Bill then promptly hung up.

Bill turned to Janet and said, "Damn, that felt good."

Janet laughed and said, "Are you really going to sue him and CNN?"

"Naw. He isn't wealthy. I just wanted him to experience a repentance moment. Let him worry for a while. CNN, however, might be a different story. But, it will come out that we didn't get married until the day after our checkin at the motel. They will claim we *were* whoring and their story would appear true, technically."

Janet laughed and said, "You know, I couldn't care less. It's totally hypocritical on their part. Do you imagine there is any married couple that didn't have sex before they got married? That's like buying a car without driving it first or buying a new pair of shoes without trying them on first."

Bill grinned and said, "I really like my new car and shoes." They broke out in laughter. "Yeah, it is hypocritical, but it gets them headlines. That's all they want. We could possibly win, but I'm not sure it's worth the trouble."

Janet turned serious and stared into Bills eyes. "Guess what, hon. We are on our honeymoon. Don't you think we should consummate our marriage?" Bill grinned.

Neither of them thought any more about the crazy world situation. Whatever was going to happen would happen without their immediate attention. They turned off their cellphones again and became totally absorbed in each other, their new life and blossoming love ... Oh yes, wild uninhabited sex, as only newlyweds experience.

They didn't turn their phones back on until the second day, well night. There were many messages, but at that moment Phil called for what must have been the last of many attempts.

"Hello, Phil. What's up?"

"Thank God I caught you. I've got the State Police looking for you. I take it you and Janet aren't watching television. We need you both ... now! There is a huge demand for the two of you. In fact, you're late. The Prophet Organization, that's what it is being called now, they have already scheduled three venues for you. You aren't going to believe this, but the first one is tonight near Austin at Kyle Field. Let me know where you are, and I will send transportation and security to deliver you there."

Bill interrupted saying, "Kyle Field? You mean the Kyle Field at College Station, the stadium for Texas AM? That is a huge stadium!"

"Yep, that's the one, and you're right. It is huge, seating capacity of 102,000 in the stands, plus additional seating in the field; and it is sold out already after only a day of advertising. I'm telling you, there is incredible interest from the general population. This whole Prophet situation has reactivated many, many dormant Christians, even some non-Christians. They are flocking to any opportunity to learn more. It's like they have been triggered on."

"Bill, I need to warn you, however, that just as many are polarizing to the other side. We all will need security from them, because they are becoming extremely outspoken and hostile. That's just the nature of the situation as it stands."

Janet said, "This is crazy."

Phil said, "Yes, even more so than I have told you. I said there are three venues. There is another scheduled in Pennsylvania at Beaver Stadium, and another for the Rose Bowl in Pasadena, California. Yes, they are huge stadiums also, and they too are sold out. Plus, these events will be televised world-wide."

Bill's face turned chalk white, but he was able to choke out, "Jesus, Phil, I don't have anything prepared. I won't be able to talk to that large of an audience."

Phil said, "Don't worry, Bill. I'll be there to interview you and Janet, along with others from our group. Before we start we will replay the videos you sent, and there will be linguists to analyze the accents, also some theologians to offer opinions.

61

All you have to do is think on your feet and respond to questions. I know you can handle that. So, just get your butts down to Austin."

By the time the phone conversation was over the State Police had found them and were knocking on their door. Luckily, they were already almost finished packing and were quickly ushered down to the rear of two waiting black Tahoes. Their SUV had a driver and two apparent security guards in dark glasses and suits. This detail looked to be FBI. Outside were two additional uniformed State Police motorcycle escorts. They also noticed that a TV news van had also found them but the reporters and camera crews were being held back by Amarillo policemen. This was really becoming surreal, and Bill and Janet seemed frozen into isolated silence.

Janet snuggled up to Bill and whispered in his ear, "What have we gotten ourselves into?"

"I have absolutely no idea, but evidently this is where we are supposed to be. Let's just go with the flow."

"But, why us?"

"I don't know my love. I guess we were chosen for this, but at least I'm glad we are together." Bill meant every word he had said, but secretly thought, *"Why me Lord? I'm not worthy. Why did you choose me? But Lord, thank you for bringing Janet into my life."*

The small caravan left immediately, being led by the motorcycle State Police, complete with flashing lights and sirens. Texas is a big state, and

Amarillo to Austin is a long distance. They thought they might be able to get a long nap en route, but as the caravan proceeded east on I-40 it suddenly turned north toward the airport then on to the runway and veered toward a Gulf Stream 5 waiting there. The involvement of the FBI was soon verified by the FBI letters stenciled on the Gulf Stream they were then escorted into.

Janet sat next to Bill, but she soon discovered that Bill was one of those that gets extremely calm in flight and sleeps. She wished she could sleep on a plane, but she was not one of those people. It wasn't a long flight, and when she felt the descent, she nudged Bill awake.

Bill stretched and asked, "Are we there?"

Janet laughed and said, "You sound like a kid, 'Are we there yet?'"

Bill was about to comment, but the Gulf Stream quickly landed and taxied off the runway toward a waiting helicopter. Three of the suits with silver shades escorted them off the plane and into the helicopter. Bill seemed to have found his voice and asked, "Why do we need a helicopter? Is the stadium that far away?"

One of the suits said, "No. We are only about fifteen minutes away, but we will be landing directly on to the field for security. The protesters are abundant and rabid. They are worse than at a Trump rally." When he saw the panic in his eyes, he continued, "Don't worry we have plenty of security there. No one can get close to you."

Bill did show panic, but not so much fear for his life, although he became seriously concerned for Janet. He didn't want her in jeopardy, but it obviously far too late to worry. No, his panic was more of shocked disbelief that the Prophet could stir up so much positive excitement and so much hate at the same time.

Bill and Janet were quickly surrounded by security as they disembarked from the helicopter. They were ushered toward a large platform constructed on the 50 yard line. As they climbed the stairs they entered into a circular clear barrier around the platform, which was presumably a bulletproof security shield. He could see Phil and several others coming to greet him, but Janet touched his arm to get his attention.

Janet said, "Listen to the silence."

Bill turned to look out over the massive crowd and listened. There were tens of thousands of people compressed tight within the huge stadium, but there was total and absolute silence within the stadium … no sound at all. The silence lay heavily on all there, especially him. It was almost as if God himself was entering the stadium. He did not like it. He did not deserve this reverence. Who were they to deserve this awe?

Phil reached him and vigorously shook his hand, then Janet's. The others were also smiling hugely and pumped his and Janet's hands. Phil guided him and Janet toward center stage chairs. Phil then turned to the audience and announced, "Reverend and Mrs. Bill Parks are now with us, and you may recognize Mrs. Parks as Dr. Janet Mercer, Mr. Harper's doctor! You will recognize them from the videos you just watched." After a moment of continued silence, the previously silent crowd exploded in a joyous roar, reverberating throughout the stadium. This stadium has heard many roars from past crowds, but this explosion would certainly top them all. It actually hurt his ears. He and Janet turned to circle around to a continuous applause and bowed to the crowd, setting them off again.

When the crowd's applause finally slowed, Phil directed Janet and Bill to seats prepared for them in the center stage area surrounded by those ready to interview them. Dr. Simpson (Phil) began, "Mr. and Mrs. Parks have agreed to be interviewed concerning the developing situation around Mr. Harper, the self-professed Prophet. We have not discussed or prepared anything previously with the Parks. You are hearing our thoughts and those of the Parks for the first time. Bill, Janet, the audience has witnessed the interviews you conducted with Mr. Harper, been read your reports and they have heard reports from our experts concerning the findings of the ancient accents and other findings, but I believe what everyone here and the millions watching on television really want to know is, do *you* believe Mr. Harper is a Prophet of God?"

Bill looked at Janet, and she looked at him. They had discussed it among themselves many times, and neither had committed to a firm belief one way or the other. But, now was the moment of truth. Bill shrugged at Janet and said, "Well, Dr. Simpson, there is nothing like just putting our feet to the fire, so to speak. But, I'm ready to answer your question ... eventually."

"I didn't know what to believe at first. Janet called me and told me she had a patient that seemed to be talking in tongues, like the Bible talks about. Mr. Harper certainly sounded like he was talking in tongues, at first anyway, until I studied what he was saying. The accent threw me off at first, but as everyone has now realized, there is a message he was conveying. It is a simple message: God's Harvest is coming soon, a message the Bible repeatedly teaches and Christians believe. I can't disagree with this basic message."

"I did some research on my own and came to a startling discovery. Allow me to provide an analogy: If Earth was a vineyard, our world population would indeed be ripe for a harvest. We are near the maximum population this world can support. Any additional population growth would only result in increasing deaths from famine, disease or wars. Again, our vineyard is at the point of harvest before the good fruit begins to wither and die."

With that statement, the huge crowd could be heard emotionally agreeing with the analogy through what sounded like a rumbling roar. Some protests were shouted out, but those were immediately silenced by the crowd, in some cases violently.

Bill continued, "Mr. Harper claimed to be Abraham, a Prophet, when he talked with the accent. Abraham talked about eternal souls, living with God, Heaven, Angels, among other biblical topics. I could not definitively disagree with anything he said. The message came to us in our own language, and simultaneously the same message came through other self-proclaimed Prophets to the world in other religions and languages with identical messages. That alone would be hard to organize and even harder to explain. That in itself seems to be a miracle. As you have seen in the videos, I asked some very pointed questions and received some very definitive responses. I accepted his answers and believed them. So, do I believe him to be Prophet?" Silence filled the pause. "Yes, I do believe Abraham and the others are, or were for a while, Prophets when they delivered their message." The crowd roared … again.

As soon as he was able he continued, "This is the first time Janet has heard me commit to believing, but Janet can speak for herself."

Janet looked at Bill, then at Dr. Simpson. After a moment of silence Janet said, "I was the first to hear Mr. Harper, and personally witnessed all the interviews. I can tell you that what was happening with Mr. Harper surpassed my understanding. It was not medical, it was something supernatural. I quickly believed Mr. Harper was exactly who he claimed to be. Yes, I believe, but I kept it a secret until just now, because

I didn't want to influence Bill." Janet then leaned over and kissed Bill.

The crowd cheered.

When the crowd calmed, Dr. Simpson said, "We have seen much to do in the news about Mr. Harper and the religious conspiracy and fraud being launched on the public, and many are blaming the two of you. It was even reported that you started the Prophet rumor to attract new members to your church, Bill. Can you comment about those reports?"

Bill actually laughed at that and said, "Well, the Prophet Abraham said that the population would polarize into good and evil. That is part of his message to us. People must decide which side they will be on. God's Harvest will be for the good only. Purge yourself of the evil. As far at the news media reports are concerned, by their action we can tell which side the majority of the news media is on." He pointed to the line of cameras, and boos erupted from the crowd. "There is far more at stake than trying to increase members of my church."

"Janet and I went to Amarillo to get married, but we heard on the news that we were there whoring. To make it worse, the Deacon of my church was on camera saying that. This was the same Deacon that also fired me as the paster. So, the polarization extends into the religious community as well. Janet was also fired from the hospital where she practiced. We know what we believe and simply ignore the attacks. Our focus now is preparing for the Harvest."

Dr. Simpson said, "The most asked questions I get concerns the Christian Bible. The King James Bible is comprised of 783,137 God inspired words. That's a lot of words, and these Prophets' words would not even come close to those of the Bible, not even a brochure. How would you explain the difference?"

"Well, I've thought a lot about that. Mr. Harper, Abraham I mean, said his message from God was simple. As you have seen, that is true; but this too is part of the message. He claims the original message has been corrupted by men in the retelling, adding to and subtracting from over the centuries. I can see how that could happen. I don't mean to imply intentional corruption, but there have been many generation of retelling. Think about it. The Prophet's message is basic and simple, but even our spoken words tonight would be added to any retelling. What would be recorded from us would only be our opinions of what we think he means, but that doesn't mean we are correct. Nevertheless, our words will become part of the message. Add many generations of added words from well-meaning religious scholars on what they believe God meant and eventually it becomes voluminous."

"Abraham was clear from the beginning that the Prophets were sent to give us the uncorrupted message from God. I believe we should accept the message solely on the actual words of the message and nothing else. The simple message is the Harvest is coming soon, so be ready. He told us how. I for one believe the message, and I plan to be ready."

Dr. Simpson said, "I can understand your explanation. Actually, it makes sense. Did you get a sense as to when the Harvest will occur?"

"Abraham said, 'Soon'. I believe he means soon. As I mentioned earlier, Earth is already ripe for a Harvest. It would be unproductive to increase the population further. I personally don't think we are talking generations, not even one. On the other hand, I don't think God would have sent a message if he wasn't giving us enough time to distribute the message and change our ways. So … your guess is as good as mine on the time frame. But, with current technology and the number of Prophets, the message is being distributed quickly. Plus, another thing to consider is the raging, hostile conflict the good versus evil polarization is causing. If it continues like we are seeing, we will be at war soon."

Silence fell heavily on the stadium. Decisions were being considered.

The other religious leaders on the dais were nodding in sudden understanding, and Dr. Simpson said, "I hadn't considered those facts, but I tend to agree. Based upon these factors I believe we must be looking at only a few years at most, maybe only months. The earliest case, possibly days."

"We've heard within the Abraham message and you have also mentioned that we need to purge the evil within ourselves. How would we go about doing that, and how long would that take?"

Bill chuckled, a sincere and comfortable tinkle of pure pleasure, and said, "Well, my training at the seminary, your teaching actually, instructs us to repent and change our ways. Our understanding of God's message in the Bible teaches us this simple message, and Abraham's message in essence says the same thing. Christians are taught that God's forgiveness is freely given, and our sins (evil) will be refined, as Abraham said, 'Purged'. It is basically a reboot of our thinking that changes us. The good in us becomes dominant."

"You must know, Phil, that I really haven't had a chance to plan these answers. I'm talking off the top of my head in secular terms to express my thoughts. I take this approach because many that hear these thoughts are not biblical scholars, some aren't even Christian. I will let others quote the scripture and verse of the Christian Bible. I'm just talking common sense. I hope this is what you want."

Those on the dais didn't have to answer. The crowd cheered ... loudly.

When the cheers died, another on the dais that had introduced himself, Dr. Freedman, said, "How do you explain the total absence of the mention of the baptism requirement. Scriptures say Repent and be Baptized."

Bill had to control his instant anger. He wasn't expecting to debate dissenting views from these gathered theologians, especially in front of this obviously secular crowd. Bill displayed no outward visible sign, but he quickly realized that

71

Dr. Freedman seemed to be polarized on the wrong side of logic and was trying to bait him to disprove Abraham's message. Bill wanted no part of that, so he thought quickly and let his mind organize. Finally Bill said, "If we assume Abraham's message *is* from God, and I do, then we must make some assumptions. Maybe Christians have made a wrong assumption about what baptism actually is. Even many of the various Christian denominations can't come up with the same definitions. Some sprinkle, some submerge the total body, still others don't even believe in baptism. Some believe baptism is only an outward testimony of an inward transformation. Abraham's message doesn't say stop baptizing, so, if you feel strongly about it, continue. I will."

Dr. Freedman said, "What about reincarnation? Christians don't believe in it.

Bill frustration continued to build, and he said, "Many religions *do* believe in reincarnation, but does it really matter? Reincarnation is what it is, and we can't control this outcome. Abraham explained how a soul never dies. Should we even try to dispute this fact?"

Dr. Freedman intended to continue with his bombardment of negative questions, but Bill raised his arms with extended open hands, stopping Dr. Freedman and said, "I don't think we want to get bogged down debating over details at this gathering. These subjects are best debated among the biblical scholars. You asked me to come here to find out if I believe the prophetic message, and I do. I think we should all make this same personal decision, and not seek an excuse to reject the message."

Dr. Freedman's face suddenly contorted in rage, and he bellowed, "I don't believe the message. Abraham is a false prophet, and I reject his lies."

Bill recoiled from the venom Dr. Freedman spewed. Silence filled the colosseum, which accented the sound of a sudden bolt of thunder from a cloudless sky, followed immediately by a bright flash of light encompassing Dr. Freedman. Dr. Freedman was there one second and gone the next. Nothing remained of him but pile of dust and smoking clothing on the dais and a floating bubble of turbulent multiple-colored energy. The energy twisted and rotated within itself and divided itself into two translucent bundles of different colors. Not quite half of the churning energy formed into a golden cloud that drifted up into the night sky and out of sight. The other more dominant cloud flamed dark red and drifted down and through the dais to disappear into the ground.

The huge crowd remained absolutely silent in shock as Janet ran to Bill to see if he was injured. After confirming he was fine, she said, "I didn't like him, anyway, and he was obviously on the wrong side. It looks like he was the first harvested, and not in the good way. Decisions do have consequences." She had meant to be heard only by Bill, but she had forgotten about the clip-on mic. The audience clearly heard what she had spoken to

Bill. The crowd reacted to her mention of the Harvest with mixed reactions. Some were shocked, some outright frightened, but those that had already made their personal decision began to cheer.

One of the FBI agents, Special Agent Cummings, ran forward looking around the dais and said to no one in particular, "Where did Dr. Freedman go?"

Bill, having mostly recovered said, "You saw what we saw. He is still here." pointing to the pile of chalk and clothing on the dais. "I believe he made his decision and was harvested."

Dr. Simpson said, "Do you believe that was a Harvest? Has it started?"

"I don't believe the general Harvest has started. I think we still have time to consider the message and repent. I think Dr. Freedman made his final and firm decision in front of the world, and God just let us know that it was a poor decision and took him, the good part anyway." Dr. Simpson just nodded in understanding.

The lead FBI agent pulled them aside, covered their microphones, and said, "Gentlemen, you have well over a hundred thousand people in attendance here and many more watching on TV. They have listened to the presentation and witnessed what has happened, and they are in near panic. I don't want to tell you your business as it relates to religion, but you better start catering to them and soon and give them some direction. If not, we could have a major crisis. I'm evacuating Bill and Janet in the helicopter, since they are the focus of these

74

gatherings. So, I'm mostly addressing you, Dr. Simpson."

Bill looked at the nervous crowd and said, "Phil, the agent is correct. These new and renewed converts need a leader, a spiritual leader. I would guess many of them have made a positive decision tonight, and they need instructions. This is especially true since they have witnessed what we believe to be a harvest. Talk to them, pray with them, advise them, and give them a direction. This is the biggest revival ever." A wide-eyed Dr. Simpson nodded in great animation.

Special Agent Cummings didn't wait for a response. He motioned two other agents to take Bill and Janet toward the helicopter. The agent led the way quickly and ushered them abroad and almost immediately they were in the air speeding away. As they left they could hear Dr. Simpson speaking to the crowd, but they couldn't decipher his words.

Bill said to the agent, "Where are we going?"

"Well, the next scheduled event is in Pennsylvania at Beaver Stadium. It's as big as this one and is smack dab in the geographical center of Pennsylvania. We are headed there now as soon as we get to the airport."

Janet said, "You are the FBI aren't you? Who is paying for all this?"

"Yes, we are the FBI. The Secret Service is also involved. This has a major potential to disrupt the country's services and infrastructure and create a national panic. We have been directed by the president to protect you and prevent any disruption. As far as who is paying for all this protection, currently it's the government; but the Christian Message group you work for has funneled huge amounts of money into funding these gatherings. The director, Dr. Simpson set this all up, and we're here to make them happen without incident. Unfortunately, we certainly had an incident tonight with Dr. Freedman."

Janet said, "Wow! This is really getting crazy, unbelievable actually. Come to think of it the whole episode has been crazy from the start."

The helicopter ride was short, retracing their route back to the waiting jet, and they were airborne almost immediately. Bill and Janet continued to be amazed at how the media, government and population seemed overly focused on them, good and bad. It shouldn't be about them. It was never about them, it was always the Prophet and message. But, the message *was* getting out, so it wasn't all bad, almost like it was planned ahead in great detail. Maybe it was.

The Gulf Stream 5 was very comfortable, and Bill and Janet were beginning to relax on the flight, when Special Agent Cummings got their attentions. He said, "You might want to watch the news. CNN is talking about the gathering at the stadium."

As Janet turned the TV monitor on she said, "I'm almost afraid to watch. CNN and us don't seem to agree on much."

As it turned out, Janet had also become a prophet. CNN's report was all negative. They were repeating over and over about the magical and theatrical disappearance of Dr. Freeman, saying it was staged to sell our false prophet story. They even had professional magicians explaining how we staged the illusion. They even offered a reward for information as to the location of Dr. Freedman. They were committed to expose our trick. They stared at the monitor in total disbelief.

Janet said, "How can they get away with telling such lies?"

Surprisingly, it was Special Agent Cummings that answered from behind them, "The media have been telling lies for years and getting away with it. They gave up reporting actual news long ago and now have their own agenda, mostly political. They make up their news, mostly lies or negative spin. That's why you hear so much about 'Fake News'. They have become totally politicized and not on our side."

Bill said, "I take it you are on our side?"

"We are supposed to remain neutral, but I'm a believer. Most on this detail are. We volunteered. But, even if I wasn't, after what I have seen and heard tonight, I would be now."

A solemn Janet asked, "Will we be safe at this next event?"

"Well, the masses desiring to attend the events will insist that they continue, but the media will have the general population agitated, those that haven't been influenced already. I will call up the military to ensure things don't get out of hand at these next two events. We will put you up at a

secret location and fly you in again by helicopter.
You will be fine."

Chapter 4
Warriors of God

They were an hour into the flight when Phil called, which Bill immediately put on speaker.

Phil knew Bill would have him on speaker and said, "You two left me in a predicament. I really wasn't prepared for over a hundred thousand staring at me looking for leadership, but it worked out well. I've seen many of the Billy Graham crusades, and he always offered an invitation at the end and thousands always came forward. Unfortunately, we didn't have the room, since the stadium was totally full, even the field. Still, many, most actually, made a decision to follow God. I just asked that those that wanted to make a commitment to raise their arms high in the air, and they did. I led them in a prayer and told them like you had said. Some believe baptism is only an outward testimony of an inward transformation. I explained that their show of hands was the outward testimony of their inward transformation, but to also seek out a church home for their personal growth. That seemed to satisfy them, but that's the best I could come up with on the spur of the moment."

"The rest of us in the group will leave quickly to get everything set up in Pennsylvania. We're glad you left when you did, we were worried about you two."

Bill said, "Phil, we're sorry about Dr. Freedman."

"Well, it is what it is. He made his choice. None of us saw that coming from him, or the Harvest for that matter. I guess it's best it happened now rather than later. Don't worry about it. We aren't."

"Thanks, Phil. We'll see you in Pennsylvania."

Janet leaned against Bill and said, "You know what, hon? I really love you, I think I loved you even before we met. We were meant to be together. And I'm so proud of you for standing up for Abraham's message. But, you have to know that I was so frightened for you when you stood up to that bully, Dr. Freedman. When that lighting struck him I thought you might have also been hurt. It scared the hell out of me, but, now that I think about it, that's probably what it was meant to do."

Bill said, "I believe God knows the heart of everyone, and he wouldn't have hurt me. He put us out front for Him, so He meant to target only Dr. Freedman, because of his definitive, poor choice."

Janet kissed him and said, "That may be true, but I bet you didn't know it was God striking him down when it happened."

Bill laughed and said, "Well, that's true, but I figured it out quick enough."

After a moment of silence Janet said, "Does this mean God is already here for the Harvest?"

"Hon, God *is* and always *has* been here. He just hasn't shown his presence very often until now.

As to the Harvest, I believe we still have some time before the final Harvest. He will surely allow some time for us to repent and change."

"Do you believe what happened to Dr. Freedman is the way it will be with everyone? I mean with the sudden light and churning, colored energy? I know that when it happens I absolutely want to be in that golden light floating up."

"I think we must assume that is the process, but who knows for sure. I want to be in that golden bubble with you my love." Bill then held her in his arms and they slept.

When they landed they were ushered into a waiting SUV and taken somewhere, they really had no idea where. It was, however, a luxury hotel; but they were unable to enjoy any of the facilities besides the quarters they were given, which were exquisite. Special Agent Cummings explained that they were far too famous and recognizable now and must remain in their room until the next evening's event.

They were both upset until Janet said, "Wow! This hotel is much better than we had on our honeymoon. Maybe we should continue our honeymoon here." They both smiled.

That's what they did: their meals were provided by room-service, they enjoyed the in-room hot-tub, saw the sights from the balcony, and spent hours in the plush, king-sized bed. They showered together in a huge shower with numerous shower-heads that seemed to massage their bodies. They enjoyed the shower so much they did it several times. Since everything was paid for, and they were living out of suitcases, they called down to the clothing store in the hotel for new clothing. It's amazing what you can get with room-service. They put all their other troubles aside and just enjoyed their honeymoon. Unfortunately, it ended all too soon.

Their evening meal was interrupted by a knock on the door. With guards on the door, they knew it had to be authorized. It was Special Agent Cummings. He entered and said, "I thought I would give you notice that we will be leaving for the stadium in an hour." Bill and Janet nodded. "Also, I've been advised that the meeting tonight will be slightly different. I understand there will be a Catholic Cardinal present on the dais with you. We don't know what to expect from that. I hate to say this, but the interview will also take a slightly different direction. There will be a talking head from CNN that will also be asking questions."

"Oh, crap!" said Janet. "This will not end well."

Agent Cummings said, "I'm afraid you could be right. Demonstrations are already occurring in most of the major cities protesting the False Prophet events, and protesters are gathering outside the stadium. But, we will have extra agents at the event. The protesters won't get inside. You will be protected."

Bill said, "Who decided to let this happen? This is an invitation for disaster? It's almost like someone is trying to set up another harvest."

82

"I agree, but from what I have been told, this was the cost to authorize and sanction the event."

Bill and Janet just shook their heads and got dressed. They were ready when the next knock came. This time there were additional agents when they were ushered down to a waiting black SUV. Motorcycle police led the way with additional SUVs in front and behind. It was a short trip to the helicopter pad and a short trip to the stadium. Like last time, they landed on the field and were escorted to the stage, accompanied by uproarious cheering from a massive crowd. Although the crowd obviously recognized them as they mounted the stage, Dr. Simpson made the introduction.

Bill and Janet waved in all direction toward the crowd. Dr. Simpson directed them to their chairs and said, "Mr. and Mrs. Parks, thanks for coming. We have already replayed the interviews with Mr. Harper (Abraham), and the other scholars have made presentations. Additionally, we have replayed the interview we conducted at the Texas stadium."

Bill and Janet stood and Bill said, "We want to thank you for your warm welcome, but we remain uncomfortable with the attention. None of this is about Janet and me. We feel that the Prophets' message should be the sole focus. We were only just involved in the initial interviews. We were asked if we believe the message, and we certainly do believe it, more so every day." The crowd roared.

Dr. Simpson said, "I'm glad you repeated your belief in the authenticity of the message, because we have additional guests that want to add to the interview with you and Janet." Phil leaned close and whispered, "Sorry, I didn't have any choice in this. Please forgive me." Bill and Janet just nodded.

Just then three men came out of a concave and started up the steps to the dais. Bill felt Janet squeeze his arm when the first one surfaced. It was none other than the abusive and obnoxious CNN reporter that blasted them at the hospital. He was also the reporter that accused him and Janet of whoring around, trying to extort funds, and got both of them fired through his negative interviews. Bill didn't know his name, nor did he want to know it, but Janet knew his name, Jim Arnet. And, now he was going to interview them. I don't think so. Still, if anyone needed to be harvested, this was the one he would route for. He knew that wasn't very Christian, but those were his thoughts, nonetheless.

The second person coming up the steps was a Catholic Cardinal completely decked out in a traditional red robe and hat. Bill considered his dress here as more theatrical, designed more to try to intimidate him and the audience. He could almost understand his purpose here, since many in the audience were, in fact, Catholic. Dr. Simpson had mentioned that very many of the lay Catholic were inclined to believe Abraham's prophecy.

Bill had no idea who the third person was, but Janet whispered, "I can't remember his name, but

I've seen him on television. He is a somewhat famous magician. As soon as Janet identified him he knew exactly why he was here.

Dr. Simpson introduced the three newcomers to the audience and to Bill and Janet. The three then all took seats facing them. At first it became a staring contest, but Bill decided to let them steer the conversation.

They didn't have to wait long. The CNN reporter began, "I wanted to face you in front of your audience. The Cardinal is here to debunk your theory of the authenticity of the false prophecy you are spouting, and I brought this professional magician to witness and debunk any more of your magical disappearing acts. I'm here to expose the fraud you two are presenting."

Bill remained calm, actually laughed in his face and said, "I really don't think you should do what you say you are going to do. You might not like the results."

The reporter interrupted, "What are you going to do? Make me disappear? I'd like to see you try."

"I don't think you do. I didn't make Dr. Freedman disappear. That was God's doing. It was as much a surprise to us as anyone else. We believe it was God's Harvest. I'm sure you don't believe that, but have you found him? I heard you have a million dollar reward to find him. Anyone claim it yet?"

85

The reporter was taken aback slightly and said, "Not yet, but they will. Cardinal Bilese, what do you have to say about this Abraham prophecy."

Cardinal Bilese said, "The Catholic church does not believe this message. We have taken the position that this is a false prophet. If God wanted to bring forth a new prophet and message it would surely come to the Catholic church through one of our many holy men. Additionally, the message itself is contrary to our teaching."

Bill said, "I'm sorry you feel that way. It is not my message, but somehow I have become the defender through no desire on my part. I have been involved since the beginning, and I do believe it to be the message from God. I hate to say it, but I find it overly arrogant for the Catholic church to reject the message just because it didn't come to the Catholic church first. I might also mention that one of the Prophets was sent specifically to the Catholic church. So, you *were* sent a Prophets, but apparently you rejected this messenger."

Cardinal Biles's face turned red and he said, "We are the protectors of Christianity. A message from God *would* come to us first. We are the chosen ones to regulate and filter the word of God, and we, and certainly I, reject this false prophet message."

Bill knew what was coming and actually recoiled from the Cardinal. Lighting struck the Cardinal and he disappeared into a cloud of dust. His red robe and hat fell to the floor and a bubble of colored energy swirled and twisted, then separated in the red and golden clouds. The gold drifted up, while the deep red sank out of sight in the floor.

The magician was all eyes. He looked all around and felt the air where the Cardinal had been. Finally, he said, "I don't know what happened, but this was no feat of magic or trickery. Whatever happened was real." The magician squealed, stumbled and ran from the stage babbling incoherently.

Those on the stage looked at each other, not initially understanding what happened, even though most had seen it before. The massive crowd remained totally silent.

Bill almost laughed when he looked at the reporter. His face was almost white. His eyes were extremely wide, and his mouth was wide open. Finally, he slammed his mouth shut and stared at Bill in sudden acceptance. He said, "This *is* for real isn't it?" Bill nodded. "Damn, I'm so, so sorry. I have been a total ass to you and Dr. Mercer. Please forgive me." After a moment of reflection Jim Arnet said, "What I said about wanting to see you make me disappear, I take back. Actually, I'm a believer now." Some in the crowd actually laughed at his reaction and statement. Those were probably already believers and hadn't cared for him in the past.

Jim Arnet got his confidence and voice back totally and turned to the audience and said, "I've had an epiphany, and I now understand I've been wrong about everything. I've also been terrible to

Mr. and Mrs. Parks, for which I sincerely apologize. I'm responsible for what happened to Cardinal Bilese. I am so sorry for what happened, which was obviously a Harvest. I mean I was sitting next to him when it happened, and it was no trick. It was real."

By this time Special Agent Cummings and others had surrounded Bill and Janet and were trying to rush them toward the helicopter. Suddenly a group of about fifteen people broke from the close crowd through the security officers and were running toward them. By their dress, some of them were the Cardinal's security and aides. A blinding bright flash encompassed many of them and they disappeared into the Harvest clouds. Two still remained standing in the midst of the dust clouds, not understanding what had happened.

That's all Bill and Janet were able to see, because they were being bodily dragged and carried toward the helicopter. They were roughly loaded aboard and in the air quickly.

Janet bellowed, "What the hell just happened?"

"I really don't know," said Bill. "I kind of saw it coming with the Cardinal. That was a planned occurrence with, what's his name, Jim Arnet? He set the Cardinal up for a harvest, but then he obviously didn't believe it was real. I dare say he does now. But, those others that were harvested, I have no idea. More confusing was the fact that not all those rushing us were harvested. I didn't understand that."

"I didn't understand any of it." Said Special Agent Cummings, "I sort of expected that CNN reporter to disappear, but I didn't see it happening with the Cardinal. I actually thought he would or should be on the side of religious enlightenment. That was a real surprise, especially those rushing the dais. All hell will break loose over all the deaths. I will have to check in with the White House to see if we go to the California event."

Janet said, "I also thought the reporter would make it happen to himself. He sure did an about face. But, I expected it with the Cardinal, since Roman Catholic hierarchy would feel threatened by a new Prophet outside of their church. The Pope has already come out against us, so the Cardinal would have to support his position, but it obviously was his thinking also or God wouldn't have taken him."

Bill said, "When will you know if we do the other event at the Rose Bowl?"

Special Agent Cummings said, "We'll take you back to the hotel, and I will let you know in the morning."

This return trip in the helicopter landed them directly on a helipad on the hotel's roof, which they found somewhat surprising. It seems their security just went up a level, but it got them to their room much faster.

The first thing they did when they got there was turn on the TV to see the news coverage of the stadium event. The coverage remained constant on CNN. Jim Arnet seemed like he was talking constantly with repeated video snips of the Harvest behind him. Jim Arnet had made a complete belief reversal. There was a video segment when Dr. Simpson invited the audience to show their repentance and acceptance of the message by raising their hands in the air, and Jim Arnet's hands were raised so high that a person would think he was trying to fly.

Jim said, "I'm a believer now. I've seen multiple Harvests, and I've seen God's Warriors in Bill and Janet Parks."

The television picture switched to a CNN panel of talking heads around a glass table, and they were now laughing at Jim Arnet. One said, "He has lost his damn mind, and we apologize to the audience." The others around the table were nodding in agreement. Another said, "They must have drugged him."

The picture switched back to a video of Jim Arnet interviewing the two surviving people that charged the stage. The two people, a husband and wife, said they just went along with the crowd when it crashed through the line of security officers. They said they were believers and just wanted to touch God's Warriors. When Jim asked them about the bolts of lighting and the floating energy, they just smiled and said, "Our hearts are right. We have repented. That's why we are still here."

Janet turned the TV off and said, "Are we God's Warriors?"

"I believe we are. God has made us his warriors whether we want it or not. I think we are serving a purpose just like Mr. Harper and even Abraham."

"We will never be able to go out in public again. We will be mobbed."

A solemn Bill said, "Darling, I don't think we will have to worry about that for long."

Janet seemed to ponder that for a while but realization registered in her eyes. Janet said, "Oh." then after a moment, "I'm scared hon."

Bill smiled and said, "This is what the message was all about, this whole thing, telling us the Harvest is coming. So, it shouldn't be a surprise. I think, for some reason, HE is calling us first; but don't be scared, we don't have anything to worry about."

Janet said, "I'm really not scared about that, it's the end of this life that's disturbing. I know it will be better on the other side, it's just not knowing how."

They were startled by a rap on their door. They looked at each other, then Bill went to the door. When he opened it Special Agent Cummings entered, followed by an entourage of others. Jim Arnet and a camera crew were among the entourage, and they began setting up for an obvious interview or at least to record the event. Knowing his arrogance he probably invited himself.

Agent Cummings said, "Sorry to burst in on you, but," pointing to another older man, "This is FBI Assistant Director Meer, my boss. Lives have been lost, and all hell is breaking loose. The Catholic Church is demanding answers and retribution."

Bill bellowed, "What do you expect me to do? I didn't do it. I don't even know what happened. It isn't like I pointed a gun at them and shot them."

Dir. Meer just as forceful said, "You knew it was going to happen didn't you?"

"After he said what he did I believed it would happen, and it did, but I didn't pull the trigger or push a button. The Prophet Abraham told us the Harvest was coming and warned us about our choices. When he publicly made his personal choice, God took him. I didn't invite the Cardinal. I didn't even know he was coming. I assume CNN brought him."

Jim Arnet said, "That true director. I set it up, but I didn't believe it would happen. I thought it was a trick, but I was wrong."

Dr. Simpson, who came in with the entourage, said, "Our group didn't know the Cardinal was coming until right before it happened. I wasn't able to tell Bill Parks until after he and Janet came on stage."

Frustrated, Dir. Meer said, "What the hell am I supposed to tell the Catholic Church?"

Bill said, "Tell them the truth: The Cardinal rejected God's message and HE Harvested him. None of you are getting it. Wake up! The Prophet's message is real! Nothing else matters. The Harvest is coming and apparently very soon. So make your own personal decision. Everyone ...

every single human on planet Earth will be Harvested. Get ready. There will not be many more tomorrows. Are you getting it now?"

After Bill finished his rant, he became surprised at the reaction. All those he had been addressing were staring at him, wide-eyed; and Dr. Simpson looked as shocked as the others, maybe even more. That in itself surprised him the most, because Phil would be the first to agree.

It was Jim Arnet that finally spoke, "See! I told you these two were God's Warriors."

Dir. Meer said, "What the hell is going on here? What's happening to them?

Jim Arnet said, "God it taking them!"

Bill and Janet turned to each other, as if to ask, "Why this reaction?" When Bill saw Janet he looked right through her. Janet was translucent, including her clothing, and slowly fading even more, but she apparently saw the same thing about Bill. Janet smiled and quickly wrapped her arms around Bill as they faded into nothingness. The space where they had been was encircled by a golden bubble that floated up, disappearing through the ceiling.

Almost as a whispered echo from a long ways away, Janet could be heard saying, "We are one and will go together as we promised."

Jim Arnet turned to his cameraman and said, "Please tell me you got all that recorded." The crew talked amount themselves and cameraman nodded.

Jim Arnet continued, "If this was a Harvest, it was completely different from the others. Their clothing disappeared also, unlike the others. I don't know what to make of it."

Dr. Simpson broke the relative silence and said, "Well, Director, we need to make a decision about the Rose Bowl event. The event is sold out, there is not another seat to be had, but we are on hold until you sign off on it. But if you don't, there could be massive complications, maybe even riots. This is California after all."

Dir. Meer's face wrinkled heavily and flushed red with the stress. Finally, he said, "After what I've seen on the various videos and especially here tonight, I'm inclined to authorize it. I have no idea what happened here in the room tonight, but I'm convinced it was supernatural. Additionally, it appears Mr. and Mrs. Parks are gone, who knows where, but gone and won't be attending the event. Without the God's Warriors to initiate what you call the Harvest, it should be safe enough."

Dr. Simpson said, "Great! I will continue with the God Warriors' work. And, Jim Arnet, I will be needing a copy of these tapes you made here tonight to play at the California event." Jim nodded.

Everyone eventually left the room, but Dr. Simpson waited all night for any sign or message to come to him. He felt extremely guilty getting Bill and Janet involved in this. The situation and building attention and pressure on them had exploded exponentially and beyond their ability to control it. They had become God's pawns in a huge chess game. God had positioned them at the lead from the start. The Prophet came to them. God uses people to spread HIS message, and both Bill and Janet spread the message very well. Obviously, God used the isolated Harvests to position and establish Bill and Janet as HIS warriors. It was a very dramatic action to reinforce HIS message to the multitudes, but, still, Bill and Janet were now gone. They weren't taken like the others, and he didn't understand why. He didn't know if they were gone for good. That's why he waited. Still, God obviously would continue to use them to reinforce HIS message in the manner they were taken, and he would certainly make sure that tape would be seen by the masses. That video would make a perfect end to the presentation at the Rose Bowl, and Bill and Janet would be there through the taped video form.

Dr. Simpson didn't know what he expected but waited in the room all night and part of the next day but nothing happened. So, he returned to his room to freshen up before going to the airport for the next leg of the presentations. This would be the last stadium event to mass crowds. Many, many people were being persuaded to make a positive decision. He hadn't even considered what would happen after this last event, maybe the full Harvest.

Phil made it to the event early, and he was glad he did, because he had to be escorted by security through the incredibly massive crowd outside that couldn't get inside. Huge television screens had been mounted on the outside for the overflow crowd. Once inside, the stadium was packed, even the field. Never had there been a crowd this large at the Rose Bowl.

He was led to the stage and cheered by the audience. The roar reverberated through the stadium. The sound probably could be heard miles away, assuming they weren't already here. The others of his team were already there seated and waiting. He went to the podium and began.

This was the third presentation he had moderated, so he made the introductions of the experts that would be making presentations. As with the other events, he made his presentation and played the videos of the interviews Bill and Janet had made of Mr. Harper and Abraham. Afterwards, the experts gathered, linguist and theologians, made their presentations. After the live and video presentations he showed the videos of the interviews of Bill and Janet at the two previous events. At the close he played the video taken in the hotel room. Of course most had seen segments of the video that had been running almost continuously on CNN, but seeing and hearing the complete interrogation in context provided far more depth. The massive audience remained in stark attention throughout.

Dr. Simpson began his closing section with an invitation of acceptance like at the others, but he was interrupted by wails from the crowd. Dr. Simpson followed the direction of the attention of the audience upwards.

Above him was a golden bubble forming in the air above the stadium lights. When it finished forming it began to slowly float down toward his position. He quickly jumped back to give it room to settle on the platform. All stared in total and absolute silence. Slowly the bright translucent bubble began to dissipate, reforming within itself into two figures taking on form. As the process continued, Dr. Simpson recognized Bill and Janet. Once the outer bubble dissipated, Bill and Janet were in solid form and clothed as they had been when they left. It was a complete reversal of the process he had witnessed in the hotel room. Unfortunately, Dr. Simpson seemed to be in shock and stood in silence, not knowing what to say.

Jim Arnet was not so inclined. He was one person that was never in loss for words. Jim ran up the steps, talking as he came. Jim said, "I was there when they were taken, and I am here when they are returned. Bill, Janet, may I ask where you have been?"

Janet said, "To answer your question, we have been with God. HE has shown us heaven, and it is wonderful. We didn't want to return, but we were told to return and tell what we have seen. God let us understand HIS nature. God is many minds and those minds are God. Since this is Earth's last opportunity to merge with HIM, HE wanted the masses of Earth to know more. There will be no additional chances. The Harvest is next."

A shocked Jim Arnet said, "Were you actually *in* heaven and with God?"

Bill said, "No. We have not yet been refined to purge our darker side. So, we were not allowed within heaven to corrupt the pure essence of good. We were only allowed to observe the beauty and nature of the soul of God and heaven. God is heaven."

"Can you tell us what it is like"

"It is beauty beyond description, intelligence and knowledge far beyond explainable, joy and happiness unobtainable or even understandable in human form. Imagine being totally satisfied and fulfilled. This is only possible after being refined (harvested), but we were allowed to experience it, if only for a short time, so we could return to try to describe it. There is no resentment, jealousy, envy, hate, pain, lust ... nothing from the dark side of our soul. There is only good, the positive side of our soul. Janet and I became one and one with all the other minds and souls ... all of us becoming part of God. God is the mental energy of infinite minds, although there are also individual minds within." Bill and Janet stared at each other and frowned at their inability to provide a detailed description. "It is frustrating, and we feel inadequate to this task. How can we explain something your mind could never conceive? As an aggravatingly poor example, how could you explain sight and colors and its beauty to someone who has been blind from birth? The same would apply to sound, taste, touch, and something as abstract as love. Having been exposed to God in this intimate way, we now feel painfully empty. We are actually now in pain with its absence and eager to be harvested and return to those wonders and become part of it."

"Did you talk to individuals there?"

"Yes and No. We communicated without words. We visited with many of our ancestors from ancient times and more recent times. They knew us and we knew them, at least the good parts that God wanted to save. We understood their lives as if we had lived them, and they lived our lives as well. We knew their memories, joy and happiness. We don't know how. It's impossible to give you a glimpse of what it is like to be there. There are no words that can explain the beauty and essence. Just trust us to tell you that there is where you want to be for eternity. Knowing what we know now, we find life here is now incredibly depressing and unfulfilled. Being absent from God is a punishment we must endure to bring this message back but hopefully not for long.

Janet wailed out in agony, quickly joined by Bill. Janet said, "God we are in agony! Please take us, now. The pain of your absence is too much to bare. Please!"

The rumble in the sky began and built to a crescendo. Suddenly the light of heaven struck Bill and Janet, rendering them to dust and smoldering clothing. A single golden bubble formed around where Bill and Janet had stood. The churning energy began within the bubble forming into the golden aura of good and the red aura of the dark side of their souls. Apparently, God had already purged much of the evil, because there was little of the red to sink below. Their golden energy floated upward, and they left the physical world together as they had promised each other.

For once in his life Jim Arnet was speechless. He stood in silence with his mouth frozen open watching Bill and Janet's conversion of the Harvest, but Dr. Simpson had regained his voice by then. He raised his hands high in the air and screamed, "Lord, take me, too. I want to be part of the Harvest." He was quickly followed by the rest of his team.

Jim Arnet's conversion was also total, and he jerked his hands in the air also and said, "Me too, God. Please take me." Simultaneously, tens of thousands in the audience also bellowed, "Take me too."

The sky immediately turned dark with rumbling and churning black clouds, and bright bolts, thousands of them, came to ground within the stadium. The stadium, inside and out, suddenly flashed in dazzling bright bolts and deafening claps of constant thunder. The stadium filled with golden bubbles drifting into the sky and smoke and the stench of ozone from the electric discharge of the lightning bolts.

When the thunder and lightning subsided, well over half of the stadium audience was gone, but Dr. Simpson, his team, and Jim Arnet were left standing dumbfounded on the dais. Dr. Simpson bellowed, "Why didn't you take us?"

Their answer came in a surprising form of a white, winged angel fluttering down from the sky to settled beside them. The angel said, *"You were not taken in this partial rapture because your tasks are not yet complete. You must tell the world what happened here tonight so the coming Harvest will be more productive. Some are slow to accept, others will never believe; but as many that will, must be made to believe for their own salvation. This is why you must remain in the flesh for a while longer. "Jim Arnet, you will be Harvested last, so you can provide the eternal witness to the end of all things"* The angel touched those on the dais on the forehead then launched again and stroked its wings, propelling into the air. It circled the stadium and spiraled slowly upward and finally out of sight above the stadium lights.

Dr. Simpson watched the angel disappear into the sky, then said to the others on the dais, "Did you feel the power surge when the angel touched you? It gave me the strength and confidence to continue."

Most of the others nodded their agreement, but Jim Arnet, no longer at a loss for words said, "Oh, yeah. I felt the energy surge into me." He then turned to the cameras and audience, about a third of the original mass, and said, "You have witnessed a miracle tonight, but you missed being a part of it. After what you have seen, how can you not believe? I was originally a major skeptic and fought the message, but somewhere during all this I became a believer. I hope you get straight before it's too late."

Dr. Simpson seemed to again recognize the fact that they were in front of a live audience and the coverage was being transmitted around the world, probably in many languages. He interrupted Jim Arnet's rant and said, "Jim, don't be so hard on the people. I don't believe those remaining that weren't harvested are not necessary nonbelievers. I'm sure many here have family at home they want to talk with before they become harvested." A cheer rose up from those in attendance. "Great. I hope that is the case, because I believe the next Harvest will not be by our request. It will come when you least expect it, but as you have heard, it will be soon. I would, suggest you get ready before that time."

Jim Arnet jumped back in and said, "Sadly, not all those remaining will be in the golden bubble. Look at the big monitor. The cameras are recording many in the stadium scrambling and fighting to steal money and valuables left behind by those taken. I don't think they got the message."

"Yes," said Dr. Simpson, "As we have been told, there are many that will never believe. Indeed, this is sad after what they have just witnessed."

Suddenly, an angry rumble could be heard in the sky, followed by many bolts of blazing and burning lighting striking those looting the departed. It could easily be seen on the monitor as they immediately burst into dust and a golden bubble, like those previously. This time the churning energy flared red with only a minor part being

102

golden. All the smaller golden bubbles slowly merged together in the air to form a single large bubble that floated out of sight. The individual red bubbles sank into the ground.

Jim Arnet said, "What just happened? This Harvest was different."

Dr. Simpson said, "I think I understand. These Harvested were evil dominant and will remain individuals in the underworld. Only the good of their souls, which was not dominant, will merge with God, but that portion will be unaware of who they once were. That is why the good merged together, since the aware soul is in the other place. Their good portions will merge with others."

"That makes sense, but it looks like no one in the audience heard us. Those that remained are all gone. I bet they are still running, expecting the lighting to hit them."

Dr. Simpson looked around to see the stadium completely empty. Even the various networks' camera crews were gone. In spite of the seriousness of the situation, Dr. Simpson laughed out loud. The security and military were nowhere to be seen, and all that was left in the stadium were Jim Arnet, his team and himself. He said, "Well, I guess we are finished here tonight.

Chapter 5
The Harvest

As they left the stadium Dr. Simpson and his team, even Jim Arnet, were almost immediately incarcerated by the FBI. They were hauled off and roughly taken to an unidentified government facility, where they were separated and placed alone in rooms, obviously for the purpose of interrogation. He had watched enough television to recognize the cameras in the corner, the simple metal table bolted to the floor, and the wall-sized mirror, obviously hiding the observers on the other side.

Dr. Simpson had been waiting alone in this interrogations room for over two hours, and from television he knew this was typical for an interrogation. It was almost comical, considering the more important issue involving God. He had done nothing wrong, so he wasn't worried. He actually didn't understand why his team had been arrested, and he hadn't been told anything. All he could do was wait, so that is what he did.

Finally, two stone-faced men in identical dark suits entered the room. The men were both well above middle-aged, so he assumed they were high level FBI Special Agents or agents from some secrete organizations no one had ever heard of. Dr. Simpson remained calm and waited. It was their show.

One of the agents said, "I'm Agent Smith and this," pointing to the other, "is Agent Jones."

Dr. Simpson thought, Yeah, right. Like I'm going to believe that. He also noted that he didn't say what agency they were from. He did, however, say, "Where is Special Agent Cummings? He has been overseeing our team and these venues."

Agent Smith said, "That's something we would also like to know. He seems to be missing along with approximately 70,000 others. Do you know what happened to them?"

"Yes, I know exactly what happened to them, and if you review the tapes from our three stadium events, especially this last one, you will know also. Half the world watched them. They can tell you. But, in case you really don't know, most of the missing are with God now."

Agent Jones said, "You said 'most'. Where are the others?

"Well, the opposite of heaven. Look down."

"You expect us to believe they went to heaven or hell?"

"Frankly, I could care less what you believe. My team and I have important work to do. If you want honest answers we can continue, but if you intend to play games, I'm leaving."

Agent Smith said, "I'm afraid you will not be allowed to leave. This is a matter of national security, and we need reasonable answers, not magical voodoo or theatrics."

"What's happening is the beginning of God's Harvest, like we have been told by His Prophets.

It's coming … soon, and it is coming for every living and dead human on Earth. There is no longer a need for national security, because there will be no nation after the Harvest. I suggest you let us go. Like I said, we have work to do."

"So do we …. uggg."

Agent Smith quickly stood, dropping his pen and note book. Dr. Simpson watched Agent Smith's face contort in what appeared to be a combination of fear and shock. His eyes went wide, and Dr. Simpson turned to see what he was looking at. Now it was his turn to register shock.

Standing inside the door was a white, translucent angel, its wings folded along his back. The door was still shut, so it must have come through the door or materialized inside the room. He was a beautiful humanoid entity, and he was smiling.

The angel spoke in riveting musical tones, impossible to ignore. He said, *"I am the Archangel Michael, God's servant, and I need my Earthly team. Their task is not yet complete."* The agents didn't or couldn't speak. *"Bring the others of my team in here immediately."*

The white-faced agents jumped to comply. They ran out the door and disappeared down the hall. The angel patiently waited, but it didn't take long. The scared agents ushered Dr. Simpson's team, including Jim Arnet, into the room. The room was full, and many other agents and guards scrambled to look in the open doorway.

Archangel Michael smiled to comfort those around him and said, *"God is coming tomorrow and will begin His Harvest. You will see God fill the sky with his golden presence. Tell the world God will blow His trumpet and send his light. When they hear the trumpet call and see His light, walk into it. These will be His valued additions. They must trust God and come into the light by faith. If some people resist and don't walk into the light, they will still be taken another day, after the main Harvest of the most desired. Those that don't have the faith and remain, risk ... well, most will not be valued by God or allowed to join him in their own identity. They will live for eternity in pain and darkness. This is what you must tell the world. This will be humanity's last chance before this planet is purged of humans, so the planet can be left to heal itself for a new Harvest."*

"I will be back tomorrow to supervise the Harvest." The Archangel Michael then faded to nothingness and was gone.

Jim Arnet bristled with excitement and said, "I will take care of this. This is what I do. Who is the head man here?" Ironically, it was Agent Smith that held up his hand. Jim nodded and said, "Are you going to help us?" Agent Smith nodded, "Do you have an auditorium in this complex?"

"Yes we do. It's on the first floor. I'll take you there now. Follow me."

Jim was already on his phone setting up a CNN camera crew to meet him in the auditorium. When they ask him the address he said, "Hell, I don't know. I was arrested and brought here, but I don't know where hear is. I must be in the LA area. Home in on my cell phone GPS and get a crew here as fast as you can." As a major reporter and commentator, Jim had lost a lot of credibility with the upper echelon at CNN, many laughing at his sudden conversion; but he had always enjoyed autonomy and major clout within the organization. This authority had not been shut down, so his request was reluctantly honored.

Jim Arnet, Dr. Simpson and his team, even the multitude of agents, entered the auditorium and began working franticly to set up the stage for a telecast and were just finishing as the CNN crew arrived.

Jim Arnet had little use or need for Dr. Simpson's team for this presentation. They were useful during the previous stadium interviews by providing certain professional evidence, but on the whole they mostly remained quiet. Jim assumed they were part of, or represented, the revenue sources. Bill, Janet, and Dr. Simpson had always been the focus, but with Bill and Janet now gone, Dr. Simpson must now be the focus. Of course, Jim Arnet would now step in to lead the presentation to the world with Dr. Simpson and his team in the background to add credibility.

Jim smiled inwardly at his brilliance and quickness of thought at having managed to overcome his initial shock and record the address of Archangel Michael, while all the others stared in disbelief. This, of course, would be the major part of his presentation.

The CNN crew arrived within thirty minutes and rushed to set up in the auditorium by Jim Arnet. Jim had been frantic to get everyone in their place and schedule the videos he planned to use in this breaking news report. When CNN announced their breaking new interruption, Jim was ready.

When the red light came on the camera Jim said, "I'm Jim Arnet, reporter for CNN, and I'm here with breaking news. This news is monumental to America and the world. I'm here to inform the world about new developments in the Prophet's Message. As many of you know, I have been covering this news from the beginning and have covered all the subsequent events at the stadiums. I'm sure most of you have seen my interviews with Rev. Bill Parks and Dr. Janet Mercer. These two have been the focus of my reports, including the stadium events. They believed and have supported the message about the coming Harvest, and we have documented actual Harvests in each of these events. For those that missed the coverage of last night's gathering at the Rose Bowl, we documented the Harvest, some call it the Rapture, of tens of thousands people including Bill and Janet. We also witnessed the presence of an angel. To recap, we will play segments of that event." The edited version was then played.

After the edited version finished playing, the red light came back on, and Jim was live again. Jim Arnet said, "What you are about to see now was recorded on my cellphone about an hour ago. As I said, this footage shows what just happened, and never before seen by anyone. Be prepared to be shocked." CNN played Jim's video.

When the red light came on this time, Jim said, "This video is real. I witnessed it myself and recorded the video. Dr. Simpson, his team, and myself were under detention and being interrogated by Agent Smith and his team about the thousands of missing people resulting from the Harvest when the angel came to us. Agent Smith, please step up and confirm what I just said."

Agent Smith, still in disbelief, stepped up beside Jim and said, "Yes, I can confirm the accuracy of what was just said. There was an actual angel that told us what to say to the world."

Jim Arnet said, "Agent Smith, you sound like one of us now." Agent Smith smiled and nodded. "Dr. Simpson, would you like to say anything?"

"Yes I would. We have been telling you for several days that the Harvest is coming, but we didn't know exactly how soon. We thought we still had some time to spread the word, but we were obviously wrong. The Harvest begins tomorrow. It is really happening, and I for one will be most eager to walk into the light. I know it's scary, because it is the unknown on the other side, but thanks to Bill and Janet, we now know what's on the other side. They were actually in pain being absent from God, but God sent them back as a sign to tell us what to look forward to. Yes, I will walk into the light, but to the rest of you, this is your last opportunity. Make a decision and be ready."

After the red light went out, everyone stood in stark silence for many long minutes, as reality seemed to settle in. Finally, Jim let out a deep breath and said, "Well, I don't think there is anything more to be done by us. CNN and all the other networks will recycle the videos of all the interviews and events, especially this last one. The word is getting out. We have done our jobs."

"On a personal note, I want to thank everyone for getting me involved. I apologize for my initial negative reporting, but I didn't believe the message. I thoroughly regret that, but my coverage brought me in contact with every aspect of the Prophet and Message. Obviously, I was converted in the process. Thank you."

"I regret that I have no family to spend these last few hours with, but I assume that the rest of you do. I suggest that you get home to them quickly."

Dr. Simpson said, "Yes, our group has a private plane here, and we will leave immediately. Jim, if you truly have no one, you are welcome to accompany us. You can wait for the Harvest with me and my family."

Jim stretched his face in a huge grin and said, "Thank you. I would love that."

They were soon in the air, racing toward the future sunrise, when the pilot announced that he was observing something strange that we might want to take a look at. They quickly looked out the windows to observe a golden glow toward the south. It was more than a glow, and it was huge, beginning to light up the entire sky.

Jim asked, "What do you suppose that is?"

Dr. Simpson said, "Well, I imagine that is the entity or essence of the body of God. I mean the angel said God was coming. My guess is it's God on approach."

Jim said, "Duh! That was a stupid question."

That's when Jim's cell phone rang. He looked at his phone and said to the others, "It's the main CNN office." He answered and listened for a while then responded, "I can't believe you people. You just don't get it. The Harvest you have been reporting is coming, and it's coming tomorrow. The light in the sky you want covered is God. I'm not going to do a report on it. Don't you understand? Nothing else matters, not my job or salary, your ratings, revenues, or anything else. Those things are all over." Jim listened more then abruptly ended the call. "Can you believe it? They want me to put together a story about the mysterious light in the sky. They would probably want me to do a story about walking into the light of the Harvest." Jim laughed.

By the time the plane landed at Will Roger's Airport in Oklahoma City, the families of Dr. Simpson and his team were waiting. Also, the golden light had completely filled the sky and dwarfed the light of the sun that was now high in the sky.

The reunited families, embraced and waited, for God was here and the time was now. Almost on cue, there sounded a deep, base blast that reverberated the very foundation of Earth. A bright spot of golden light struck the ground near their group. It seemed like a personal and private light and invitation just for them.

Jim Arnet watched Dr. Simpson link hands with his wife and children, some grown with children of their own, and walk toward the beam. They walked with confidence and faith into their eternal future. Once within the light they burst into dust and their golden bubbles raced toward the huge golden glow above. They were quickly followed by others, and Jim could imagine this happening all over the globe. He took a deep breath and walked into the light with his newly found faith but nothing happened.

Jim stood in the light for long moments, with no effect. For a moment he panicked, thinking God wasn't going to take him. Why not? He was a believer. Suddenly, he remembered the angels' message to him, *"You will be the last to be Harvested. You will bear witness to the end of all things on Earth."*

"Oh crap!" he thought, *"God's not going to take me yet. My task is not yet complete."* Jim said out loud, "I might as well call CNN for an affiliate here and do their report. That's the best place to observe the activities around the world."

Dr. Simpson had left his keys in his car. He certainly knew he wouldn't need the car anymore.

Jim drove to the address provided by CNN. The CNN studio had already been geared up to accommodate his needs before he arrived. They were obviously short-staffed, which made him feel better. At least some of the organization were believers and had walked into the light. Sadly, however, there were far too many nonbelievers still working, like there would be a tomorrow. Maybe he could enlighten some of them.

Jim went immediately to the communication complex to find out what was happening around the world. The news coverage was reporting millions, maybe even billions around the world have disappeared by walking into the light. Some captions read "Mass Suicide." Other captions read "Contagious Disillusions Sweep the World." None of the captions mentioned God in anything but negative terms, they didn't even use a capital G. Jim smiled to himself, knowing that he would soon be left alone in a world of nonbelievers, probably even committed evil souls. Few would be on his side now, even here at CNN. But, he knew where he would be soon. Maybe, just maybe he could convert more before he left.

The many monitors continued to cycle through major cities throughout the world with golden lights. The feeds were live and in real time. The videos showed a continuous flow of calm people voluntarily walking into the light by faith and disappearing into golden bubbles.

Jim had been an agnostic all his life, possibly even a committed atheist. He had always said that it would take a burning bush to make him believe in God, like Moses had encountered on Mt. Horeb. But, he had seen many burning bushes in the last few days, and now he believed. He believed with all his heart and repented and asked for forgiveness, and he had many sins to be forgiven for. Never would he have believed that one day he would be preaching for conversion, but that is exactly what he was doing and what he intended to do now.

When the red light came on the camera he stood in front of and spoke, "Ladies and gentlemen still at home watching TV I say to you: What the hell are you doing still at home. Why aren't you out rushing to the golden light while it is still shining? I walked into the light several hours ago, but my Harvest has been delayed. An angel informed me that I was chosen to witness the end of all things. So, here I am bearing witness through our instant technology. I'm watching millions of every religion walk into the light and are now with God. Our Prophet told us that the world population would polarize into good and evil, and it appears that is exactly what is happening."

"I have been an agnostic all my life, but I now believe. If you have been following my reports you know I have seen the miracles. You have seen them. I have seen God's Warriors, angels, and I will see God soon. Ladies and gentlemen, this is no trick, this is real. Why don't you believe?"

"In the remote chance that you have not seen my reports, we will replay them for you with my personal commentary. Please listen carefully, and I

115

hope you will believe. This is your last chance, because the golden light will eventually end, along with any hope for you. The next Harvest will come for you and your hosted souls within you. Those souls within you will be judged by whatever they have made of themselves. You are luckier than them, because you have this one final chance to make the right decision. God will take you whether you want it or not, and He will send you to a place you will not want to be, and you will be there for eternity. My strong advice to you is get up off your ass right now and walk into the light."

Some creative engineer had activated an automatic counting method to project those entering the golden light from the various cities being monitored. It wouldn't be accurate but provided an estimated count. The continuous increasing count was superimposed on the bottom of the screen. It was already indicating over a billion. It was labeled "Death Count". Jim just shook his head in disgust. CNN would be biased and negative to the very end.

The replays began, beginning with the initial video of Mr. Harper. There was no need to provide live comments, and after a few of the videos Jim stopped trying. He had lived them and believed them, so he reverted to offering his comments at the end. The stadium events were quite lengthy, and by the end of the first event in Texas, he noticed the slowing of the supposed "Death Count" and became aware that the end of lines could be seen. Jim knew the first Harvest was nearing its end and broke in to the CNN transmission to announce these facts. Sadly, the numbers reported were far from representing anything near the world population. If the numbers were anywhere close, less than 60% of the population had walked into the light. How could there be so many rejecting God?

By the end of the recorded event in Pennsylvania, most of the monitors showed empty lines. The golden lights continued for about 30 minutes without people entering them, then they began to shut down until there were no more. Jim cringed, knowing the end of all things was imminent.

Jim's attention was drawn to the monitors by bellows from the attendants. When he looked he saw the video feeds were switching to view a dark ominous looking cloud building. It was the same on all the monitors from around the world. He couldn't tell in what direction, but apparently it was approaching from every direction. The cloud expanded into a huge darkness filling the golden sky. Within the turbulent cloud churned violent lighting that began striking the earth is sheets. It was yet too far away from any of the cameras recording it to tell the effect on the ground, but Jim knew it was the second Harvest beginning.

The cloud spread out across the horizon and moved forward. As it came closer, he could now see that the sheets of lighting were striking people running ahead to it. Terrible fear could be seen gripping the faces of the people as they vaporized. He watched the video images as the storm reached and passed the camera. Behind the storm nothing had been harmed except the people, of which there were none. All that could be seen were golden and deep red bubbles floating up and down. Nothing else moved behind the storm.

He heard it first: the rumble of the storm, the continuous booms of the lighting, the screams of the people trying to run away. He then saw the horrible explosions of the bodies around him. The toxic smell of burning flesh and ozone from the lighting assaulted his nostrils. Then it passed, and he still remained. Amazed, he looked around and he was alone. No sign of life could be detected on any of the monitors, that surprisingly still worked. Why? Why do I remain. The Harvest must be complete. What am I now to witness?

Jim wandered up to the roof to look around through his own eyes. When he opened the door and walked out on the observation deck he was struck with wonder. Except for the golden light, he noticed with amazement the clearest and bluest sky he had ever seen … ever. There was no smog at all. The air was pristine, like it had never been polluted. There was no sign of the storm anywhere. It was like the Harvest had purified Earth. He could even smell wild flowers growing, somewhere. He saw birds flying and, in the total silence, he heard dogs barking from a long ways away. Great, the Harvest apparently hadn't destroyed animal life, only humans.

Now he understood. Earth had been purified. He now remembered Abraham saying that Earth would be left to heal itself for the next Harvest. This is what he was meant to witness.

As Jim was enjoying the overwhelming sense of peace and quiet, a voice from behind him almost sent him over the edge of the building. The voice said, "Hello Jim Arnet."

Jim quickly grabbed the railing and spun around. There standing looking at him were Bill and Janet. They were dressed in white robs holding hands and smiling at him. Jim said, "I didn't expect to see you two on Earth again. What are you doing here?"

Bill said, "We didn't expect to be here again, but God isn't through with us here, and He sent up back. We are evidently here, along with some chosen others, to repopulate Earth for the next Harvest."

Janet said, "We always felt that God brought us together, and we now know why. He said we were chosen from the beginning to be His Warriors, to be the focus of spreading His message, and be part of the repopulation."

Jim said, "Well you two *were* certainly the focus for sure. I must ask, do you resent at all being sent back?"

Bill said, "Not really. We have witnessed Heaven and will miss it, but compared to eternity, completing our lives and tasks on Earth is but a blink of the eye. We know what is waiting for us, so we are happy to experience of life. It will be rewarding to us."

Jim said, "Since I am still here, am I to stay here also?"

The Archangel Michael fluttered down beside him, smiling. He said, *"No, Jim Arnet, you have witnessed what God wanted you to see. Your task is complete, and it is time to go."* Michael then touched Jim on the forehead and he felt himself transforming. He welcomed seeing his sins float away in the red bubble, as he floated up with Michael. What a story he could tell.

The End